"What's up?" inquired the other.

"'Ere's my old woman coming now," said the skipper. "Sent a note to say she's getting ready as fast as she can, an' I'm not to sail on any account till she comes."

"That's awkward," said the mate, who felt that he was expected to say something.

"It never struck me to tell her your wife was coming," said the skipper. "Where we're to put 'em both I don't know. I s'pose it's quite certain your wife'll come?"

"Certain," said the mate.

"No chance of 'er changing 'er mind?" suggested the skipper, looking away from him.

"Not now she's got that bonnet," replied the mate. "I s'pose there's no chance of your wife changing hers?"

The skipper shook his head. "There's one thing," he said hopefully, "they'll be nice company for each other. They'll have to 'ave the state-room between 'em. It's a good job my wife ain't as big as yours."

"We'll be able to play four 'anded wist sometimes," said the mate, as he followed the skipper below to see what further room could be made.

"Crowded, but jolly," said the other.

The two cabs drove up almost at the same moment while they were below, and Mrs. Bunnett's cabman had no sooner staggered on to the jetty with her luggage than Mrs. Fillson's arrived with hers.

The two ladies, who were entire strangers, stood regarding each other curiously as they looked down at the bare deck of the Foam.

"George!" cried Mrs. Fillson, who was a fine woman, raising her voice almost to a scream in the effort to make herself heard above the winch of a neighbouring steamer.

It was unfortunate perhaps that both officers of the schooner bore the same highly-respectable Christian name.

"George!" cried Mrs. Bunnett, glancing indignantly at the other lady.

"Ge-orge!" cried Mrs. Fillson, returning her looks with interest.

"Hussy," said Mrs. Bunnett under her breath, but not very much under.

"George!"

There was no response.

"George!" cried both ladies together.

Still no response, and they made a louder effort

There was yet another George on board, in the forecastle, and, in response to pushes from curious friends below, he came up, and regarded the fair duettists open-mouthed.

"What d'yer want?" he said at length sheepishly.

"Will you tell Captain Bunnett that his wife, Mrs. Bunnett, is here?" said that lady, a thin little woman with bright black eyes.

"Yes, mum," said the seaman, and was hurrying off when Mrs. Fillson called him back.

"Will you tell Mr. Fillson that his wife, Mrs. Fillson, is up here?" she said politely.

"All right, mum," said the other, and went below to communicate the pleasing tidings. Both husbands came up on deck hastily, and a glance served to show them how their wives stood.

"How do you do, Cap'n Bunnett," said Mrs. Fill-son, with a fascinating smile.

"Good-morning, marm," said the skipper, trying to avoid his wife's eye; "that's my wife, Mrs. Bunnett."

"Good-morning, ma'am," said Mrs. Fillson, adjusting the new bonnet with the tips of her fingers.

"Good-morning to you," said Mrs. Bunnett in a cold voice, and patronising. "You have come to bring your husband some of his things, I suppose?"

"She's coming with us," said the skipper, in a hurry to have it over. "Wait half a moment, and I'll help you down."

He got up on to the side and helped them both to the deck, and, with a great attempt at cheery conversation, led the way below, where, in the midst of an impressive silence, he explained that the ladies would have to share the state-room between them.

"That's the only way out of it," said the mate, after waiting in vain for them to say something.

"It's a fairish size when you come to look at it," said the skipper, putting his head on one side to see whether the bunk looked larger that way.

"Pack three in there at a pinch," said the mate hardily.

Still the ladies said nothing, but there was a storm-signal hoisted in Mrs. Bunnett's cheek, which boded no good to her husband. There was room only for one trunk in the state-room, and by prompt generalship Mrs. Fillson got hers in first. Having seen it safe she went up on deck, for a look round.

"George," said Mrs. Bunnett fiercely, as soon as they were alone.

"Yes, my dear," said her husband.

"Pack that woman off home," said Mrs. Bunnett sharply.

W.W. JACOBS – THE SHORT STORIES
VOLUME 2

William Wymark Jacobs was born on September 8th, 1863 in the Wapping district of London, England. Jacobs grew up near the docks, where his father was a wharf manager. The docks and river side would be a constant theme of his writing in years to come.

Although surrounded by poverty, he received a formal education in London, first at a private prep school and later at the Birkbeck Literary and Scientific Institute.

His working life began with a less than exciting clerical position at the Post Office Savings Bank. Jacobs put his imagination to good use writing short stories, sketches and articles, many for the Post Office house publication "Blackfriars Magazine."

In 1896 Jacobs published Many Cargoes, a selection of sea-faring yarns, which established him as a popular writer with a knack for authentic dialogue and trick endings.

A year later he published a novelette, The Skipper's Wooing, and in 1898 another collection of short stories; Sea Urchins. These works painted vivid pictures of dockland and seafaring London full of colourful characters.

By 1899, Jacobs was able to quit the post office and write full-time.

He married the noted suffragist Agnes Eleanor Williams (who had been jailed for her protest activities) in 1900. They set up households both in Loughton, Essex and in central London.

The publication in 1902 of At Sunwich Port and Dialstone Lane, in 1904, cemented Jacobs' reputation as one of the leading British authors of the new century.

There followed a string of further successful publications, including Captain's All (1905), Night Watches (1914), The Castaways (1916), and Sea Whispers (1926).

Though Jacobs would create little in the way of new work after 1911, he still wrote and was recognized as a leading humorist, ranked alongside such writers as P. G. Wodehouse.

William Wymark Jacobs died in a North London nursing home in Hornsey Lane, Islington on September 1st, 1943.

Index of Contents

A RASH EXPERIMENT

The hands on the wharf had been working all Saturday night and well into the Sunday morning to finish the Foam, and now, at ten o'clock, with hatches down and freshly-scrubbed decks, the skipper and mate stood watching the tide as it rose slowly over the smooth Thames mud.

"What time's she coming?" inquired the skipper, turning a lazy eye up at the wharf.

"About ha'-past ten she said," replied the mate. "It's very good o' you to turn out and let her have your state-room."

"Don't say another word about that," said the skipper impressively. "I've met your wife once or twice, George, an' I must say that a nicer spoken woman, an' a more well-be'aved one, I've seldom seen."

"Same to you," said the mate; "your wife I mean."

"Any man," continued the skipper, "as would lay in a comfortable state-room, George, and leave a lady a-trying to turn and to dress and ondress herself in a poky little locker, ought to be ashamed of himself."

"You see, it's the luggage they bring," said the mate, slowly refilling his pipe. "What they want with it all I can't think. As soon as my old woman makes up her mind to come for a trip, tomorrow being Bank Holiday, an' she being in the mind for a outing, what does she do?' Goes down Commercial Road and buys a bonnet far beyond her station."

"They're all like it," said the skipper; "mine's just as bad. What does that boy want?"

The boy approached the edge of the jetty, and, peering down at them, answered for himself.

"Who's Captain Bunnett?" he demanded shrilly.

"That's me, my lad," said the skipper, looking up.

"I've got a letter for yer," said the boy, holding it out.

The skipper held out his hands and caught it; and, after reading the contents, felt his beard and looked at the mate.

"It never rains but it pours," he said figuratively.

"I couldn't do that," said the skipper firmly. "It's your own fault; you should have said you was coming."

"Oh, I know you didn't want me to come," said Mrs. Bunnett, the roses on her bonnet trembling. "The mate can think of a little pleasure for his wife, but I can stay at home and do your mending and keep the house clean. Oh, I know; don't tell me."

"Well, it's too late to alter it," said her husband. "I must get up above now; you'd better come too."

Mrs. Bunnett followed him on deck, and, getting as far from the mate's wife as possible, watched with a superior air of part ownership the movements of the seamen as they got under way. A favourable westerly breeze was blowing, and the canvas once set she stood by her husband as he pointed out the various objects of interest on the banks of the river.

They were still in the thick of the traffic at dinner-time, so that the skipper was able, to his secret relief, to send the mate below to do the honours of the table. He came up from it pale and scared, and, catching the skipper's eye, hunched his shoulders significantly.

"No words?" inquired the latter anxiously, in a half-whisper.

"Not exactly words," replied the mate. "What you might call snacks."

"I know," said the other with a groan.

"If you don't now," said the mate, "you will at tea-time. I'm not going to sit down there with them alone again. You needn't think it If you was to ask me what I've been eating I couldn't tell you."

He moved off a bit as his table companions came up on deck, and the master of the Foam deciding to take the bull by the horns, called both of them to him, and pointed out the beauties of the various passing craft. In the midst of his discourse his wife moved off, leaving the unhappy man conversing alone with Mrs. Fillson, her face containing an expression such as is seen in the prints of the very best of martyrs as she watched them.

At tea-time the men sat in misery; Mrs. Bunnett passed Mrs. Fillson her tea without looking at her, an example which Mrs. Fillson followed in handing her the cut bread and butter. When she took the plate back it was empty, and Mrs. Bunnett, convulsed with rage, was picking the slices out of her lap.

"Oh, I am sorry," said Mrs. Fillson.

"You're not, ma'am," said Mrs. Bunnett fiercely. "You did it a purpose."

"There, there!" said both men feebly.

"Of course my husband'll sit quite calm and see me insulted," said Mrs. Bunnett, rising angrily from her seat.

"And my husband'll sit still drinking tea while I'm given the lie," said Mrs. Fillson, bending an indignant look upon the mate.

"If you think I'm going to share the state-room with that woman, George, you're mistaken," said Mrs. Bunnett in a terrible voice. "I'd sooner sleep on a doorstep."

"And I'd sooner sleep on the scraper," said Mrs. Fillson, regarding her foe's scanty proportions.

"Very well, me an' the mate'll sleep there," said the skipper wearily. "You can have the mate's bunk and Mrs. Fillson can have the locker. You don't mind, George?"

"Oh, George don't mind," said Mrs. Bunnett mimickingly; "anything'll do for George. If you'd got the spirit of a man, you wouldn't let me be insulted like this."

"And if you'd got the spirit of a man," said Mrs. Fillson, turning on her husband, "you wouldn't let them talk to me like this. You never stick up for me."

She flounced up on deck where Mrs. Bunnett, after a vain attempt to finish her tea, shortly followed her. The two men continued their meal for some time in silence.

"We'll have to 'ave a quarrel just to oblige them, George," said the skipper at length, as he put down his cup. "Nothing else'll satisfy 'em."

"It couldn't be done," said the mate, reaching over and clapping him on the back.

"Just pretend, I mean," said the other.

"It couldn't be done proper," said the mate; "they'd see through it. We've sailed together five years now, an' never 'ad what I could call a really nasty word."

"Well, if you can think o' anything," said the skipper, "say so. This sort o' thing is worrying."

"See how we get on at breakfast," said the mate, as he lit his pipe. "If that's as bad as this, we'll have a bit of a row to please 'em."

Breakfast next morning was, if anything, worse, each lady directly inciting her lord to acts of open hostility. In this they were unsuccessful, but in the course of the morning the husbands arranged matters to their own satisfaction, and at the next meal the storm broke with violence.

"I don't wish to complain or hurt anybody's feelings," said the skipper, after a side-wink at the mate, "but if you could eat your wittles with a little less noise, George, I'd take it as a favour."

"Would you?" said the mate, as his wife stiffened suddenly in her seat. "Oh!"

Both belligerents, eyeing each other ferociously, tried hard to think of further insults.

"Like a pig," continued the skipper grumblingly.

The mate hesitated so long for a crushing rejoinder that his wife lost all patience and rose to her feet crimson with wrath.

"How dare you talk to my husband like that?" she demanded fiercely. "George, come up on deck this instant!"

"I don't mind what he says," said the mate, who had only just begun his dinner.

"You come away at once," said his wife, pushing his plate from him.

The mate got up with a sigh, and, meeting the look of horror-stricken commiseration in his captain's eye, returned it with one of impotent rage.

"Use a larger knife, cap'n," he said savagely. "You'll swallow that little 'un one of these days."

The skipper, with the weapon in question gripped in his fist, turned round and stared at him in petrified amazement, "If I wasn't the cap'n o' this ship, George," he said huskily, "an' bound to set a good example to the men, I'd whop you for them words."

"It's all for your good, Captain Bunnett," said Mrs. Fillson mincingly. "There was a poor old workhouse man I used to give a penny to sometimes, who would eat with his knife, and he choked himself with it."

"Ay, he did that, and he hadn't got a mouth half the size o' yours," said the mate warningly.

"Cap'n or no cap'n, crew or no crew," said the skipper in a suffocating voice, "I can't stand this. Come up on deck, George, and repeat them words."

Before the mate could accept the invitation, he was dragged back by his wife, while at the same time Mrs. Bunnett, with a frantic scream, threw her arms round her husband's neck, and dared him to move.

"You wait till I get you ashore, my lad," said the skipper threateningly.

"I'll have to bring the ship home after I've done with you," retorted the mate as he passed up on deck with his wife.

During the afternoon the couples exchanged not a word, though the two husbands exchanged glances of fiery import, and later on, their spouses being below, gradually drew near to each other. The mate, however, had been thinking, and as they came together met his foe with a pleasant smile.

"Bravo, old man," he said heartily.

"What d'yer mean?" demanded the skipper in gruff astonishment.

"I mean the way you pretended to row me," said the mate. "Splendid you did it. I tried to back you up, but lor! I wasn't in it with you."

"What, d'yer mean to say you didn't mean what you said?" inquired the other.

"Why, o' course," said the mate with an appearance of great surprise. "You didn't, did you?"

"No," said the skipper, swallowing something in his throat. "No, o' course not But you did it well, too, George. Uncommon well, you did."

"Not half so well as you did," said the mate. "Well, I s'pose we've got to keep it up now."

"I s'pose so," said the skipper; "but we mustn't keep it up on the same things, George. Swallerin' knives an' that sort o' thing, I mean."

"No, no," said the mate hastily.

"An' if you could get your missus to go home by train from Summercove, George, we might have a little peace and quietness," added the other.

"She'd never forgive me if I asked her," said the mate; "you'll have to order it, cap'n."

"I won't do that, George," said the skipper firmly. "I'd never treat a lady like that aboard my ship. I 'ope I know 'ow to behave myself if I do eat with my knife."

"Stow that," said the mate, reddening. "We'll wait an' see what turns up," he added hopefully.

For the next three days nothing fresh transpired, and the bickering between the couples, assumed on the part of the men and virulent on the part of their wives, went from bad to worse. It was evident that the ladies preferred it to any other amusement life on ship-board could offer, and, after a combined burst of hysterics on their part, in which the whole ship's company took a strong interest, the husbands met to discuss heroic remedies.

"It's getting worse and worse," said the skipper ruefully. "We'll be the laughing-stock o' the crew even afore they're done with us. There's another day afore we reach Summercove, there's five or six days there, an' at least five back again."

"There'll be murder afore then," said the mate, shaking his head.

"If we could only pack 'em both 'ome by train," continued the skipper.

"That's an expense," said the mate.

"It 'ud be worth it," said the other.

"An' they wouldn't do it," said the mate, "neither of 'em."

"I've seen women having rows afore," said the skipper, "but then they could get away from each other. It's being boxed up in this little craft as does the mischief."

"S'pose we pretend the ship's not seaworthy," said the mate.

"Then they'd stand by us," said the skipper, "closer than ever."

"I b'leeve they would," said the mate. "They'd go fast enough if we'd got a case o' small-pox or anything like that aboard, though."

The skipper grunted assent.

"It 'ud be worth trying," said the mate. "We've pretended to have a quarrel. Now just as we're going into port let one of the hands, the boy if you like, pretend he's sickening for small-pox."

"How's he going to do it?" inquired the skipper derisively.

"You leave it to me," replied the other. "I've got an idea how it's to be done."

Against his better judgment the skipper, after some demur, consented, and the following day, when the passengers were on deck gazing at the small port of Summercove as they slowly approached it, the cook came up excitedly and made a communication to the skipper.

"What?" cried the latter. "Nonsense."

"What's the matter?" demanded Mrs. Bunnett, turning round.

"Cook, here, has got it into his head that the boy's got the small-pox," said the skipper.

Both women gave a faint scream.

"Nonsense," said Mrs. Bunnett, with a pale face.

"Rubbish," said Mrs. Fillson, clasping her hands nervously.

"Very good, mum," said the cook calmly. "You know best, o' course, but I was on a barque once what got it aboard bad, and I think I ought to know it when I see it."

"Yes; and now you think everything's the smallpox," said Mrs. Bunnett uneasily.

"Very well, mum," said the cook, spreading out his hands. "Will you come down an' 'ave a look at 'im?"

"No," snapped Mrs. Bunnett, retreating a pace or two.

"Will you come down an' 'ave a look at 'im, sir," inquired the cook.

"You stay where you are, George," said Mrs. Bunnett shrilly, as her husband moved forward. "Go farther off, cook."

"And keep your tongue still when we get to port," said the mate. "Don't go blabbing it all over the place, mind, or we shan't get nobody to work us out."

"Ay, ay," said the cook, moving off. "I ain't afraid of it—I've given it to people, but I've never took it myself yet."

"I'm sure I wish I was off this dreadful ship," said Mrs. Fillson nervously. "Nothing but unpleasantness. How long before we get to Summercove, Cap'n Bunnett?"

"'Bout a hour an' a 'arf ought to do it," said the skipper.

Both ladies sighed anxiously, and, going as far aft as possible, gazed eagerly at the harbour as it opened out slowly before them.

"I shall go back by train," said Mrs. Bunnett. "It's a shame, having my holiday spoilt like this."

"It's one o' them things what can't be helped," said her husband piously.

"You'd better give me a little money," continued his wife. "I shall get lodgings in the town for a day or two, till I see how things are going."

"It 'ud be better for you to get straight back home," said the skipper.

"Nonsense," said his wife sharply. "Suppose you take it yourself, I should have to be here to see you were looked after. I'm sure Mrs. Fillson isn't going home."

Mrs. Fillson, holding out her hand to Mr. Fillson, said she was sure she wasn't.

"It 'ud be a load off our minds if you did go," said the mate, speaking for both.

"Well, we're not going for a day or two at any-rate," said Mrs. Bunnett, glancing almost amiably at Mrs. Fillson.

In face of this declaration, and in view of the persistent demands of the ladies, both men, with a very ill grace furnished them with some money.

"Don't say a word about it ashore, mind," said the mate, avoiding his chief's indignant gaze.

"But you must have a doctor," said Mrs. Bunnett.

"I know of a doctor here," said the mate; "that's all arranged for."

He moved away for a little private talk with the skipper, but that gentleman was not in a conversational mood, and a sombre silence fell upon all until they were snugly berthed at Summercove, and the ladies, preceded by their luggage on a trolly, went off to look for lodgings. They sent down an hour later to say that they had found them, and that they were very clean and comfortable, but a little more than they had intended to give. They implored their husbands not to run any unnecessary risks, and sent some disinfectant soap for them to wash with.

For three days they kept their lodgings and became fast friends, going, despite their anxiety, for various trips in the neighbourhood. Twice a day at least they sent down beef-tea and other delicacies for the invalid, which never got farther than the cabin, communication being kept up by a small boy who had strict injunctions not to go aboard. On the fourth day in the early morning they came down as close to the ship as they dared to bid farewell.

"Write if there's any change for the worse," cried Mrs. Bunnett.

"Or if you get it, George," cried Mrs. Fillson anxiously.

"It's all right, he's going on beautiful," said the mate.

The two wives appeared to be satisfied, and with a final adieu went off to the railway station, turning at every few yards to wave farewells until they were out of sight.

"If ever I have another woman aboard my ship, George," said the skipper, "I'll run into something. Who's the old gentleman?"

He nodded in the direction of an elderly man with white side-whiskers, who, with a black bag in his hand, was making straight for the schooner.

"Captain Bunnett?" he inquired sharply.

"That's me, sir," said the skipper.

"Your wife sent me," said the tall man briskly. "My name's Thompson—Dr. Thompson. She says you've got a case of small-pox on board which she wants me to see."

"We've got a doctor," said the skipper and mate together.

"So your wife said, but she wished me particularly to see the case," said Dr. Thompson. "It's also my duty as the medical officer of the port."

"You've done it, George, you've done it," moaned the panic-stricken skipper reproachfully.

"Well, anybody can make a mistake," whispered the mate' back; "an' he can't touch us, as it ain't small-pox. Let him come, and we'll lay it on to the cook. Say he made a mistake."

"That's the ticket," said the skipper, and turned to assist the doctor to the deck as the mate hurried below to persuade the indignant boy to strip and go to bed.

In the midst of a breathless silence the doctor examined the patient; then, to the surprise of all, he turned to the crew and examined them one after the other.

"How long has this boy been ill?" he demanded.

"About four days," said the puzzled skipper.

"You see what comes of trying to hush this kind of thing up," said the doctor sternly. "You keep the patient down here instead of having him taken away and the ship disinfected, and now all these other poor fellows have got it."

"What?" screamed the skipper, as the crew broke into profane expressions of astonishment and self-pity. "Got what?"

"Why, the small-pox," said the doctor. "Got it in its worst form too. Suppressed. There's not one of them got a mark on him. It's all inside."

"Well, I'm damned," said the skipper, as the crew groaned despairingly.

"What else did you expect?" inquired the doctor wrathfully. "Well, they can't be moved now; they must all go to bed, and you and the mate must nurse them."

"And s'pose we catch it?" said the mate feelingly.

"You must take your chance," said the doctor; then he relented a little. "I'll try to send a couple of nurses down this afternoon," he added. "In the meantime you must do what you can for them."

"Very good sir," said the skipper brokenly.

"All you can do at present," said the doctor, as he slowly mounted the steps, "is to sponge them all over with cold water. Do it every half-hour till the rash comes out."

"Very good," said the skipper again. "But you'll hurry up with the nurses, sir!"

He stood in a state of bewilderment until the doctor was out of sight, and then, with a heavy sigh, took his coat off and set to work.

He and the mate, after warning off the men who had come down to work, spent all the morning in sponging their crew, waiting with an impatience born of fatigue for the rash to come out. This impatience was shared by the crew, the state of mind of the cook after the fifth sponging calling for severe rebuke on the part of the skipper.

"I wish the nurses 'ud come, George," he said, as they sat on the deck panting after their exertions; "this is a pretty mess if you like."

"Seems like a judgment," said the mate wearily.

"Halloa, there," came a voice from the quay.

Both men turned and looked up at the speaker.

"Halloa," said the skipper dully.

"What's all this about small-pox?" demanded the new-comer abruptly.

The skipper waved his hand languidly towards the forecastle.

"Five of 'em down with it," he said quietly. "Are you another doctor, sir?"

Without troubling to reply, their visitor jumped on board and went nimbly below, followed by the other two.

"Stand out of the light," he said brusquely. "Now, my lads, let's have a look at you."

He examined them in a state of bewilderment, grunting strangely as the washed-out men submitted to his scrutiny.

"They've had the best of cold sponging," said the skipper, not without a little pride.

"Best of what?" demanded the other.

The skipper told him, drawing back indignantly as the doctor suddenly sat down and burst into a hoarse roar of laughter. The unfeeling noise grated harshly on the sensitive ears of the sick men, and Joe Burrows, raising himself in his bunk, made a feeble attempt to hit him.

"You've been sold," said the doctor, wiping his eyes.

"I don't take your meaning," said the skipper with dignity.

"Somebody's been having a joke with you," said the doctor. "Get up, you fools; you've got about as much small-pox as I have."

"Do you mean to tell me—" began the skipper.

"Somebody's been having a joke with you, I tell you," repeated the doctor, as the men, with sundry oaths, half of relief, half of dudgeon, got out of bed and began groping for their clothes. "Who is it, do you think?"

The skipper shook his head, and the mate, following his lead, in duty bound, shook his; but a little while after, as they sat by the wheel smoking and waiting for the men to return to work the cargo out, they were more confidential. The skipper removed his pipe from his mouth, and, having eyed the mate for some time in silence, jerked his thumb in the direction of the railway station. The mate, with a woe-begone nod, assented.

A SAFETY MATCH

Mr. Boom, late of the mercantile marine, had the last word, but only by the cowardly expedient of getting out of earshot of his daughter first, and then hurling it at her with a voice trained to compete with hurricanes. Miss Boom avoided a complete defeat by leaning forward with her head on one side in the attitude of an eager but unsuccessful listener, a pose which she abandoned for one of innocent joy when her sire, having been deluded into twice repeating his remarks, was fain to relieve his overstrained muscles by a fit of violent coughing.

"I b'lieve she heard it all along," said Mr. Boom sourly, as he continued his way down the winding lane to the little harbour below. "The only way to live at peace with wimmen is to always be at sea; then they make a fuss of you when you come home—if you don't stay too long, that is."

He reached the quay, with its few tiny cottages, and brown nets spread about to dry in the sun, and walking up and down, grumbling, regarded with jaundiced eye a few small smacks which lay in the harbour, and two or three crusted amphibians lounging aimlessly about.

"Mornin', Mr. Boom," said a stalwart youth in sea-boots, appearing suddenly over the edge of the quay from his boat.

"Mornin', Dick," said Mr. Boom affably; "just goin' off?"

"'Bout an hour's time," said the other: "Miss Boom well, sir?"

"She's a' right," said Mr. Boom; "me an' her 've just had a few words. She picked up something off the floor what she said was a cake o' mud off my heel. Said she wouldn't have it," continued Mr. Boom, his voice rising. "My own floor too. Swep' it up off the floor with a dustpan and brush, and held it in front of me to look at."

Dick Tarrell gave a grunt which might mean anything—Mr. Boom took it for sympathy.

"I called her old maid," he said with gusto; "'you're a fidgety old maid,' I said. You should ha' seen her look. Do you know what I think, Dick?"

"Not exactly," said Tarrell cautiously.

"I b'leeve she's that savage that she'd take the first man that asked her," said the other triumphantly; "she's sitting up there at the door of the cottage, all by herself."

Tarrell sighed.

"With not a soul to speak to," said Mr. Boom pointedly.

The other kicked at a small crab which was passing, and returned it to its native element in sections.

"I'll walk up there with you if you're going that way," he said at length.

"No, I'm just having a look round," said Mr. Boom, "but there's nothing to hinder you going, Dick, if you've a mind to."

"There's no little thing you want, as I'm going there, I s'pose?" suggested Tarrell. "It's awkward when you go there and say, 'Good-morning,' and the girl says, 'Good-morning,' and then you don't say any more and she don't say any more. If there was anything you wanted that I could help her look for, it 'ud make talk easier."

"Well—go for my baccy pouch," said Mr. Boom, after a minute's thought, "it'll take you a long time to find that."

"Why?" inquired the other.

"'Cos I've got it here," said the unscrupulous Mr. Boom, producing it, and placidly filling his pipe.

"You might spend—ah—the best part of an hour looking for that."

He turned away with a nod, and Tarrell, after looking about him in a hesitating fashion to make sure that his movements were not attracting the attention his conscience told him they deserved, set off in the hang-dog fashion peculiar to nervous lovers up the road to the cottage. Kate Boom was sitting at the door as her father had described, and, in apparent unconsciousness of his approach, did not raise her eyes from her book. "Good-morning," said Tarrell, in a husky voice.

Miss Boom returned the salutation, and, marking the place in her book with her forefinger, looked over the hedge on the other side of the road to the sea beyond.

"Your father has left his pouch behind, and being as I was coming this way, asked me to call for it," faltered the young man.

Miss Boom turned her head, and, regarding him steadily, noted the rising colour and the shuffling feet.

"Did he say where he had left it?" she inquired.

"No," said the other.

"Well, my time's too valuable to waste looking for pouches," said Kate, bending down to her book again, "but if you like to go in and look for it, you may!"

She moved aside to let him pass, and sat listening with a slight smile as she heard him moving about the room.

"I can't find it," he said, after a pretended search.

"Better try the kitchen now then," said Miss Boom, without looking up, "and then the scullery. It might be in the woodshed or even down the garden. You haven't half looked."

She heard the kitchen door close behind him, and then, taking her book with her, went upstairs to her room. The conscientious Tarrell, having duly searched all the above-mentioned places, returned to the parlour and waited. He waited a quarter of an hour, and then going out by the front door, stood irresolute.

"I can't find it," he said at length, addressing himself to the bedroom window.

"No. I was coming down to tell you," said Miss Boom, glancing sedately at him from over the geraniums. "I remember seeing father take it out with him this morning."

Tarrell affected a clumsy surprise. "It doesn't matter," he said. "How nice your geraniums are."

"Yes, they're all right," said Miss Boom briefly.

"I can't think how you keep 'em so nice," said Tarrell.

"Well, don't try," said Miss Boom kindly. "You'd better go back and tell father about the pouch. Perhaps he's waiting for a smoke all this time."

"There's no hurry," said the young man; "perhaps he's found it."

"Well, I can't stop to talk," said the girl; "I'm busy reading."

With these heartless words she withdrew into the room, and the discomfited swain, only too conscious of the sorry figure he cut, went slowly back to the harbour, to be met by Mr. Boom with a wink of aggravating and portentous dimensions.

"You've took a long time," he said slyly. "There's nothing like a little scheming in these things."

"It didn't lead to much," said the discomfited Tarrell.

"Don't be in a hurry, my lad," said the elder man, after listening to his experiences. "I've been thinking over this little affair for some time now, an' I think I've got a plan."

"If it's anything about baccy pouches—" began the young man ungratefully.

"It ain't," interrupted Mr. Boom, "it's quite diff'rent Now, you'd best get aboard your craft and do your duty. There's more young men won girls' 'arts while doing of ther duty than—than—if they wasn't doing their duty. Do you understand me?"

It is inadvisable to quarrel with a prospective father-in-law, so that Tarrell said he did, and with a moody nod tumbled into his boat and put off to the smack. Mr. Boom having walked up and down a bit, and exchanged a few greetings, bent his steps in the direction of the "Jolly Sailor," and, ordering two mugs of ale, set them down on a small bench opposite his old friend Raggett.

"I see young Tarrell go off grumpy-like," said Raggett, drawing a mug towards him and gazing at the fast-receding boats.

"Ay, we'll have to do what we talked about," said Boom slowly. "It's opposition what that gal wants. She simply sits and mopes for the want of somebody to contradict her."

"Well, why don't you do it?" said Raggett. "That ain't much for a father to do surely."

"I hev," said the other slowly, "more than once. O' course, when I insist upon a thing, it's done; but a woman's a delikit creeter, Raggett, and the last row we had she got that ill that she couldn't get up to get my breakfast ready, no, nor my dinner either. It made us both ill, that did."

"Are you going to tell Tarrell?" inquired Raggett.

"No," said his friend. "Like as not he'd tell her just to curry favour with her. I'm going to tell him he's not to come to the house no more. That'll make her want him to come, if anything will. Now there's no use wasting time. You begin to-day."

"I don't know what to say," murmured Raggett, nodding to him as he raised the beer to his lips.

"Just go now and call in—you might take her a nosegay."

"I won't do nothing so damned silly," said Raggett shortly.

"Well, go without 'em," said Boom impatiently; "just go and get yourselves talked about, that's all— have everybody making game of both of you, talking about a good-looking young girl being sweethearted by an old chap with one foot in the grave and a face like a dried herring. That's what I want."

Mr. Raggett, who was just about to drink, put his mug down again and regarded his friend fixedly.

"Might, I ask who you're alloodin' to?" he inquired somewhat shortly.

Mr. Boom, brought up in mid-career, shuffled a little and laughed uneasily. "Them ain't my words, old chap," he said; "it was the way she was speaking of you the other day."

"Well, I won't have nothin' to do with it," said Raggett, rising.

"Well, nobody needn't know anything about it," said Boom, pulling him down to his seat again. "She won't tell, I'm sure—she wouldn't like the disgrace of it."

"Look here," said Raggett, getting up again.

"I mean from her point of view," said Mr. Boom querulously; "you're very 'asty, Raggett."

"Well, I don't care about it," said Raggett slowly; "it seemed all right when we was talking about it; but s'pose I have all my trouble for nothing, and she don't take Dick after all? What then?"

"Well, then there's no harm done," said his friend, "and it 'll be a bit o' sport for both of us. You go up and start, an' I'll have another pint of beer and a clean pipe waiting for you against you come back."

Sorely against his better sense Mr. Raggett rose and went off, grumbling. It was fatiguing work on a hot day, climbing the road up the cliff, but he took it quietly, and having gained the top, moved slowly towards the cottage.

"Morning, Mr. Raggett," said Kate cheerily, as he entered the cottage. "Dear, dear, the idea of an old man like you climbing about! It's wonderful."

"I'm sixty-seven," said Mr. Raggett viciously, "and I feel as young as ever I did."

"To be sure," said Kate soothingly; "and look as young as ever you did. Come in and sit down a bit."

Mr. Raggett with some trepidation complied, and sitting in a very upright position, wondered how he should begin. "I am just sixty-seven," he said slowly. "I'm not old and I'm not young, but I'm just old enough to begin to want somebody to look after me a bit."

"I shouldn't while I could get about if I were you," said the innocent Kate. "Why not wait until you're bed-ridden?"

"I don't mean that at all," said Mr. Raggett snappishly. "I mean I'm thinking of getting married."

"Good—gracious!" said Kate, open-mouthed.

"I may have one foot in the grave, and resemble a dried herring in the face," pursued Mr. Raggett with bitter sarcasm, "but—"

"You can't help that," said Kate gently.

"But I'm going to get married," said Raggett savagely.

"Well, don't get in a way about it," said the girl. "Of course, if you want to, and—and—you can find somebody else who wants to, there's no reason why you shouldn't! Have you told father about it?"

"I have," said Mr. Raggett, "and he has given his consent."

He put such meaning into this remark, and so much more in the contortion of visage which accompanied it, that the girl stood regarding him in blank astonishment.

"His consent?" she said in a strange voice.

Mr. Raggett nodded.

"I went to him first," he said, trying to speak confidently. "Now I've come to you—I want you to marry me!"

"Don't you be a silly old man, Mr. Raggett," said Kate, recovering her composure. "And as for my father, you go back and tell him I want to see him."

She drew aside and pointed to the door, and Mr. Raggett, thinking that he had done quite enough for one day, passed out and retraced his steps to the "Jolly Sailor." Mr. Boom met him half-way, and having received his message, spent the rest of the morning in fortifying himself for the reception which awaited him.

It would be difficult to say which of the two young people was the more astonished at this sudden change of affairs. Miss Boom, pretending to think that her parent's reason was affected, treated him accordingly, a state of affairs not without its drawbacks, as Mr. Boom found to his cost Tarrell, on the other hand, attributed it to greed, and being forbidden the house, spent all his time ashore on a stile nearly opposite, sullenly watching events.

For three weeks Mr. Raggett called daily, and after staying to tea, usually wound up the evening by formally proposing for Kate's hand. Both conspirators were surprised and disappointed at the quietness with which Miss Boom received these attacks; Mr. Raggett meeting with a politeness which was a source of much wonder to both of them.

His courting came to an end suddenly. He paused one evening with his hand on the door, and having proposed in the usual manner, was going out, when Miss Boom called him back.

"Sit down, Mr. Raggett," she said calmly. Mr. Raggett, wondering inwardly, resumed his seat.

"You have asked me a good many times to marry you," said Kate.

"I have," said Mr. Raggett, nodding.

"And I'm sure it's very kind of you," continued the girl, "and if I've hurt your feelings by refusing you, it is only because I have thought perhaps I was not good enough for you."

In the silence which followed this unexpected and undeserved tribute to Mr. Raggett's worth, the two old men eyed each other in silent consternation.

"Still, if you've made up your mind," continued the girl, "I don't know that it's for me to object. You're not much to look at, but you've got the loveliest chest of drawers and the best furniture all round in Mastleigh. And I suppose you've got a little money?"

Mr. Raggett shook his head, and in a broken voice was understood to say: "A very little."

"I don't want any fuss or anything of that kind," said Miss Boom calmly. "No bridesmaids or anything of that sort; it wouldn't be suitable at your age."

Mr. Raggett withdrew his pipe and holding it an inch or two from his mouth, listened like one in a dream.

"Just a few old friends, and a bit of cake," continued Miss Boom musingly. "And instead of spending a lot of money in foolish waste, we'll have three weeks in London."

Mr. Raggett made a gurgling noise in his throat, and suddenly, remembering himself, pretended to think that it was something wrong with his pipe, and removing it blew noisily through the mouthpiece.

"Perhaps," he said, in a trembling voice—"perhaps you'd better take a little longer to consider, my dear."

Kate shook her head. "I've quite made up my mind," she said, "quite. And now I want to marry you just as much as you want to marry me. Good-night, father; good-night—George."

Mr. Raggett started violently, and collapsed in his chair.

"Raggett," said Mr. Boom huskily.

"Don't talk to me," said the other, "I can't bear it."

Mr. Boom, respecting his friend's trouble, relapsed into silence again, and for a long time not a word was spoken.

"My 'ed's in a whirl," said Mr. Raggett at length.

"It 'ud be a wonder if it wasn't," said Mr. Boom sympathetically.

"To think," continued the other miserably, "how I've been let in for this. The plots an' the plans and the artfulness what's been goin' on round me, an' I've never seen it."

"What d'ye mean?" demanded Mr. Boom, with sudden violence.

"I know what I mean," said Mr. Raggett darkly.

"P'raps you'll tell me then," said the other.

"Who thought of it first?" demanded Mr. Raggett ferociously. "Who came to me and asked me to court his slip of a girl?"

"Don't you be a old fool," said Mr. Boom heatedly. "It's done now, and what's done can't be undone. I never thought to have a son-in-law seven or eight years older than what I am, and what's more, I don't want it."

"Said I wasn't much to look at, but she liked my chest o' drawers," repeated Raggett mechanically.

"Don't ask me where she gets her natur' from, cos I couldn't tell you," said the unhappy parent; "she don't get it from me."

Mr. Raggett allowed this reflection upon the late Mrs. Boom to pass unnoticed, and taking his hat from the table fixed it firmly upon his head, and gazing with scornful indignation upon his host, stepped slowly out of the door without going through the formality of bidding him good-night.

"George," said a voice from above him.

Mr. Raggett started, and glanced up at somebody leaning from the window.

"Come in to tea to-morrow early," said the voice pressingly; "good-night, dear."

Mr. Raggett turned and fled into the night, dimly conscious that a dark figure had detached itself from the stile opposite, and was walking beside him.

"That you, Dick?" he inquired nervously, after an oppressive silence.

"That's me," said Dick. "I heard her call you 'dear.'" Mr. Raggett, his face suffused with blushes, hung his head.

"Called you 'dear,'" repeated Dick; "I heard her say it. I'm going to pitch you in the harbour. I'll learn you to go courting a young girl. What are you stopping for?"

Mr. Raggett delicately intimated that he was stopping because he preferred, all things considered, to be alone. Finding the young man, however, bent upon accompanying him, he divulged the plot of which he had been the victim, and bitterly lamented his share in it.

"You don't want to marry her then?" said the astonished Dick.

"Course I don't," snarled Mr. Raggett; "I can't afford it. I'm too old; besides which, she'll turn my little place topsy-turvy. Look here, Dick, I done this all for you. Now, it's evident she only wants my furniture: if I give all the best of it to you, she'll take you instead."

"No, she won't," said Dick grimly; "I wouldn't have her now, not if she asked me on her bended knee."

"Why not?" said Raggett.

"I don't want to marry that sort o' girl," said the other scornfully; "it's cured me."

"What about me then?" said the unfortunate Raggett.

"Well, so far as I can see it serves you right for mixing in other people's business," said Dick shortly. "Well, good-night, and good luck to you."

To Mr. Raggett's sore disappointment he kept to his resolution, and being approached by Mr. Boom on his elderly friend's behalf, was rudely frank to him.

"I'm a free man again," he said blithely, "and I feel better than I've felt for ever so long. More manly."

"You ought to think of other people," said Mr. Boom severely; "think of poor old Raggett."

"Well, he's got a young wife out of it," said Dick. "I daresay he'll be happy enough. He wants somebody to help him spend his money."

In this happy frame of mind he resumed his ordinary life, and when he encountered his former idol, met her with a heartiness and unconcern which the lady regarded with secret disapproval. He was now so sure of himself that, despite a suspicion of ulterior design on the part of Mr. Boom, he even accepted an invitation to tea.

The presence of Mr. Raggett made it a slow and solemn function, Nobody with any feelings could eat with an appetite with that afflicted man at the table, and the meal passed almost in silence. Kate cleared the meal away, and the men sat at the open door with their pipes while she washed up in the kitchen.

"Me an' Raggett thought o' stepping down to the 'Sailor,'" said Mr. Boom, after a third application of his friend's elbow.

"I'll come with you," said Dick.

"Well, we've got a little business to talk about," said Boom confidentially; "but we sha'n't be long. If you wait here, Dick, we'll see you when we come back."

"All right," said Tarrell.

He watched the two old men down the road, and then, moving his chair back into the room, silently regarded the busy Kate.

"Make yourself useful," said she brightly; "shake the tablecloth."

Tarrell took it to the door, and having shaken it, folded it with much gravity, and handed it back.

"Not so bad for a beginner," said Kate, taking it and putting it in a drawer. She took some needlework from another drawer, and, sitting down, began busily stitching.

"Wedding-dress?" inquired Tarrell, with an assumption of great ease.

"No, tablecloth!" said the girl, with a laugh.

"You'll want to know a little more before you get married."

"Plenty o' time for me," said Tarrell; "I'm in no hurry."

The girl put her work down and looked up at him.

"That's right," she said staidly. "I suppose you were rather surprised to hear I was going to get married?"

"A little," said Tarrell; "there's been so many after old Raggett, I didn't think he'd ever be caught."

"Oh!" said Kate.

"I daresay he'll make a very good husband," said Tarrell patronisingly. "I think you'll make a nice couple. He's got a nice home."

"That's why I'm going to marry him," said Kate. "Do you think it's wrong to marry a man for that?"

"That's your business," said Tarrell coldly. "Speaking for myself, and not wishing to hurt your feelings, I shouldn't like to marry a girl like that."

"You mean you wouldn't like to marry me?" said Kate softly.

She leaned forward as she spoke, until her breath fanned his face.

"That's what I do mean," said Tarrell, with a suspicion of doggedness in his voice.

"Not even if I asked you on my bended knees?" said Kate. "Aren't you glad you're cured?"

"Yes," said Tarrell manfully.

"So am I," said the girl; "and now that you are happy, just go down to the 'Jolly Sailor,' and make poor old Raggett happy too."

"How?" asked Tarrell.

"Tell him that I have only been having a joke with him," said Kate, surveying him with a steady smile. "Tell him that I overheard him and father talking one night, and that I resolved to give them both a lesson. And tell them that I didn't think anybody could have been so stupid as they have been to believe in it."

She leaned back in her chair, and, regarding the dumbfounded Tarrell with a smile of wicked triumph, waited for him to speak. "Raggett, indeed!" she said disdainfully.

"I suppose," said Tarrell at length, speaking very slowly, "my being stupid was no surprise to you?"

"Not a bit," said the girl cheerfully.

"I'll ask you to tell Raggett yourself," said Tarrell, rising and moving towards the door. "I sha'n't see him. Good-night."

"Good-night," said she. "Where are you going, then?"

There was no reply.

"Where are you going?" she repeated. Then a suspicion of his purpose flashed across her. "You're not foolish enough to be going away?" she cried in dismay.

"Why not?" said Tarrell slowly.

"Because," said Kate, looking down—"oh, because—well, it's ridiculous. I'd sooner have you stay here and feel what a stupid you've been making of yourself. I want to remind you of it sometimes."

"I don't want reminding," said Tarrell, taking Raggett's chair; "I know it now."

A SPIRIT OF AVARICE

Mr. John Blows stood listening to the foreman with an air of lofty disdain. He was a free-born Englishman, and yet he had been summarily paid off at eleven o'clock in the morning and told that his valuable services would no longer be required. More than that, the foreman had passed certain strictures upon his features which, however true they might be, were quite irrelevant to the fact that Mr. Blows had been discovered slumbering in a shed when he should have been laying bricks.

"Take your ugly face off these 'ere works," said the foreman; "take it 'ome and bury it in the back-yard. Anybody'll be glad to lend you a spade."

Mr. Blows, in a somewhat fluent reply, reflected severely on the foreman's immediate ancestors, and the strange lack of good-feeling and public spirit they had exhibited by allowing him to grow up.

"Take it 'ome and bury it," said the foreman again. "Not under any plants you've got a liking for."

"I suppose," said Mr. Blows, still referring to his foe's parents, and now endeavouring to make excuses for them—"I s'pose they was so pleased, and so surprised when they found that you was a 'uman being, that they didn't mind anything else."

He walked off with his head in the air, and the other men, who had partially suspended work to listen, resumed their labours. A modest pint at the Rising Sun revived his drooping spirits, and he walked home thinking of several things which he might have said to the foreman if he had only thought of them in time.

He paused at the open door of his house and, looking in, sniffed at the smell of mottled soap and dirty water which pervaded it. The stairs were wet, and a pail stood in the narrow passage. From the kitchen came the sounds of crying children and a scolding mother. Master Joseph Henry Blows, aged three, was "holding his breath," and the family were all aghast at the length of his performance. He re-covered it as his father entered the room, and drowned, without distressing himself, the impotent efforts of the others. Mrs. Blows turned upon her husband a look of hot inquiry.

"I've got the chuck," he said, surlily.

"What, again?" said the unfortunate woman. "Yes, again," repeated her husband.

Mrs. Blows turned away, and dropping into a chair threw her apron over her head and burst into discordant weeping. Two little Blows, who had ceased their outcries, resumed them again from sheer sympathy.

"Stop it," yelled the indignant Mr. Blows; "stop it at once; d'ye hear?"

"I wish I'd never seen you," sobbed his wife from behind her apron. "Of all the lazy, idle, drunken, good-for-nothing—"

"Go on," said Mr. Blows, grimly.

"You're more trouble than you're worth," declared Mrs. Blows. "Look at your father, my dears," she continued, taking the apron away from her face; "take a good look at him, and mind you don't grow up like it."

Mr. Blows met the combined gaze of his innocent offspring with a dark scowl, and then fell to moodily walking up and down the passage until he fell over the pail. At that his mood changed, and, turning fiercely, he kicked that useful article up and down the passage until he was tired.

"I've 'ad enough of it," he muttered. He stopped at the kitchen-door and, putting his hand in his pocket, threw a handful of change on to the floor and swung out of the house.

Another pint of beer confirmed him in his resolution. He would go far away and make a fresh start in the world. The morning was bright and the air fresh, and a pleasant sense of freedom and adventure possessed his soul as he walked. At a swinging pace he soon left Gravelton behind him, and, coming to the river, sat down to smoke a final pipe before turning his back forever on a town which had treated him so badly.

The river murmured agreeably and the rushes stirred softly in the breeze; Mr. Blows, who could fall asleep on an upturned pail, succumbed to the influence at once; the pipe dropped from his mouth and he snored peacefully.

He was awakened by a choking scream, and, starting up hastily, looked about for the cause. Then in the water he saw the little white face of Billy Clements, and wading in up to his middle he reached out and, catching the child by the hair, drew him to the bank and set him on his feet. Still screaming with terror, Billy threw up some of the water he had swallowed, and without turning his head made off in the direction of home, calling piteously upon his mother.

Mr. Blows, shivering on the bank, watched him out of sight, and, missing his cap, was just in time to see that friend of several seasons slowly sinking in the middle of the river. He squeezed the water from his trousers and, crossing the bridge, set off across the meadows.

His self-imposed term of bachelorhood lasted just three months, at the end of which time he made up his mind to enact the part of the generous husband and forgive his wife everything. He would not go into details, but issue one big, magnanimous pardon.

Full of these lofty ideas he set off in the direction of home again. It was a three-days' tramp, and the evening of the third day saw him but a bare two miles from home. He clambered up the bank at the side of the road and, sprawling at his ease, smoked quietly in the moonlight.

A waggon piled up with straw came jolting and creaking toward him. The driver sat dozing on the shafts, and Mr. Blows smiled pleasantly as he recognised the first face of a friend he had seen for three months. He thrust his pipe in his pocket and, rising to his feet, clambered on to the back of the waggon, and lying face downward on the straw peered down at the unconscious driver below.

"I'll give old Joe a surprise," he said to himself. "He'll be the first to welcome me back."

"Joe," he said, softly. "'Ow goes it, old pal?"

Mr. Joe Carter, still dozing, opened his eyes at the sound of his name and looked round; then, coming to the conclusion that he had been dreaming, closed them again.

"I'm a-looking at you, Joe," said Mr. Blows, waggishly. "I can see you."

Mr. Carter looked up sharply and, catching sight of the grinning features of Mr. Blows protruding over the edge of the straw, threw up his arms with a piercing shriek and fell off the shafts on to the road. The astounded Mr. Blows, raising himself on his hands, saw him pick himself up and, giving vent to a series of fearsome yelps, run clumsily back along the road.

"Joe!" shouted Mr. Blows. "J-o-o-oE!"

Mr. Carter put his hands to his ears and ran on blindly, while his friend, sitting on the top of the straw, regarded his proceedings with mixed feelings of surprise and indignation.

"It can't be that tanner 'e owes me," he mused, "and yet I don't know what else it can be. I never see a man so jumpy."

He continued to speculate while the old horse, undisturbed by the driver's absence, placidly continued its journey. A mile farther, however, he got down to take the short cut by the fields.

"If Joe can't look after his 'orse and cart," he said, primly, as he watched it along the road, "it's not my business."

The footpath was not much used at that time of night, and he only met one man. They were in the shadow of the trees which fringed the new cemetery as they passed, and both peered. The stranger was satisfied first and, to Mr. Blows's growing indignation, first gave a leap backward which would not have disgraced an acrobat, and then made off across the field with hideous outcries.

"If I get 'old of some of you," said the offended Mr. Blows, "I'll give you something to holler for."

He pursued his way grumbling, and insensibly slackened his pace as he drew near home. A remnant of conscience which had stuck to him without encouragement for thirty-five years persisted in suggesting that he had behaved badly. It also made a few ill-bred inquiries as to how his wife and children had subsisted for the last three months. He stood outside the house for a short space, and then, opening the door softly, walked in.

The kitchen-door stood open, and his wife in a black dress sat sewing by the light of a smoky lamp. She looked up as she heard his footsteps, and then, without a word, slid from the chair full length to the floor.

"Go on," said Mr. Blows, bitterly; "keep it up. Don't mind me."

Mrs. Blows paid no heed; her face was white and her eyes were closed. Her husband, with a dawning perception of the state of affairs, drew a mug of water from the tap and flung it over her. She opened her eyes and gave a faint scream, and then, scrambling to her feet, tottered toward him and sobbed on his breast.

"There, there," said Mr. Blows. "Don't take on; I forgive you."

"Oh, John," said his wife, sobbing convulsively, "I thought you was dead. I thought you was dead. It's only a fortnight ago since we buried you!"

"Buried me?" said the startled Mr. Blows. "Buried me?"

"I shall wake up and find I'm dreaming," wailed Mrs. Blows; "I know I shall. I'm always dreaming that you're not dead. Night before last I dreamt that you was alive, and I woke up sobbing as if my 'art would break."

"Sobbing?" said Mr. Blows, with a scowl. "For joy, John," explained his wife.

Mr. Blows was about to ask for a further explanation of the mystery when he stopped, and regarded with much interest a fair-sized cask which stood in one corner.

"A cask o' beer," he said, staring, as he took a glass from the dresser and crossed over to it. "You don't seem to 'ave taken much 'arm during my—my going after work."

"We 'ad it for the funeral, John," said his wife; "leastways, we 'ad two; this is the second."

Mr. Blows, who had filled the glass, set it down on the table untasted; things seemed a trifle uncanny.

"Go on," said Mrs. Blows; "you've got more right to it than anybody else. Fancy 'aving you here drinking up the beer for your own funeral."

"I don't understand what you're a-driving at," retorted Mr. Blows, drinking somewhat gingerly from the glass. 'Ow could there be a funeral without me?"

"It's all a mistake," said the overjoyed Mrs. Blows; "we must have buried somebody else. But such a funeral, John; you would ha' been proud if you could ha' seen it. All Gravelton followed, nearly. There was the boys' drum and fife band, and the Ancient Order of Camels, what you used to belong to, turned out with their brass band and banners—all the people marching four abreast and sometimes five."

Mr. Blows's face softened; he had no idea that he had established himself so firmly in the affections of his fellow-townsmen.

"Four mourning carriages," continued his wife, "and the—the hearse, all covered in flowers so that you couldn't see it 'ardly. One wreath cost two pounds."

Mr. Blows endeavoured to conceal his gratification beneath a mask of surliness. "Waste o' money," he growled, and stooping to the cask drew himself an-other glass of beer.

"Some o' the gentry sent their carriages to follow," said Mrs. Blows, sitting down and clasping her hands in her lap.

"I know one or two that 'ad a liking for me," said Mr. Blows, almost blushing.

"And to think that it's all a mistake," continued his wife. "But I thought it was you; it was dressed like you, and your cap was found near it."

"H'm," said Mr. Blows; "a pretty mess you've been and made of it. Here's people been giving two pounds for wreaths and turning up with brass bands and banners because they thought it was me, and it's all been wasted."

"It wasn't my fault," said his wife. "Little Billy Clements came running 'ome the day you went away and said 'e'd fallen in the water, and you'd gone in and pulled 'im out. He said 'e thought you was drownded, and when you didn't come 'ome I naturally thought so too. What else could I think?"

Mr. Blows coughed, and holding his glass up to the light regarded it with a preoccupied air.

"They dragged the river," resumed his wife, "and found the cap, but they didn't find the body till nine weeks afterward. There was a inquest at the Peal o' Bells, and I identified you, and all that grand funeral was because they thought you'd lost your life saving little Billy. They said you was a hero."

"You've made a nice mess of it," repeated Mr. Blows.

"The rector preached the sermon," continued his wife; "a beautiful sermon it was, too. I wish you'd been there to hear it; I should 'ave enjoyed it ever so much better. He said that nobody was more surprised than what 'e was at your doing such a thing, and that it only showed 'ow little we knowed our fellow-creatures. He said that it proved there was good in all of us if we only gave it a chance to come out."

Mr. Blows eyed her suspiciously, but she sat thinking and staring at the floor.

"I s'pose we shall have to give the money back now," she said, at last.

"Money!" said the other; "what money?"

"Money that was collected for us," replied his wife. "One 'undered and eighty-three pounds seven shillings and fourpence."

Mr. Blows took a long breath. "Ow much?" he said, faintly; "say it agin."

His wife obeyed.

"Show it to me," said the other, in trembling tones; "let's 'ave a look at it. Let's 'old some of it."

"I can't," was the reply; "there's a committee of the Camels took charge of it, and they pay my rent and allow me ten shillings a week. Now I s'pose it'll have to be given back?"

"Don't you talk nonsense," said Mr. Blows, violently. "You go to them interfering Camels and say you want your money—all of it. Say you're going to Australia. Say it was my last dying wish."

Mrs. Blows puckered her brow.

"I'll keep quiet upstairs till you've got it," continued her husband, rapidly. "There was only two men saw me, and I can see now that they thought I was my own ghost. Send the kids off to your mother for a few days."

His wife sent them off next morning, and a little later was able to tell him that his surmise as to his friends' mistake was correct. All Gravelton was thrilled by the news that the spiritual part of Mr. John Blows was walking the earth, and much exercised as to his reasons for so doing.

"Seemed such a monkey trick for 'im to do," complained Mr. Carter, to the listening circle at the Peal o' Bells. "'I'm a-looking at you, Joe,' he ses, and he waggled his 'ead as if it was made of india-rubber."

"He'd got something on 'is mind what he wanted to tell you," said a listener, severely; "you ought to 'ave stopped, Joe, and asked 'im what it was."

"I think I see myself," said the shivering Mr. Carter. "I think I see myself."

"Then he wouldn't 'ave troubled you anymore," said the other.

Mr. Carter turned pale and eyed him fixedly. "P'r'aps it was only a death-warning," said another man.

"What d'ye mean, 'only a death-warning'?" demanded the unfortunate Mr. Carter; "you don't know what you're talking about."

"I 'ad an uncle o' mine see a ghost once," said a third man, anxious to relieve the tension.

"And what 'appened?" inquired the first speaker. "I'll tell you after Joe's gone," said the other, with rare consideration.

Mr. Carter called for some more beer and told the barmaid to put a little gin in it. In a pitiable state of "nerves" he sat at the extreme end of a bench, and felt that he was an object of unwholesome interest to his acquaintances. The finishing touch was put to his discomfiture when a well-meaning friend in a vague and disjointed way advised him to give up drink, swearing, and any other bad habits which he might have contracted.

The committee of the Ancient Order of Camels took the news calmly, and classed it with pink rats and other abnormalities. In reply to Mrs. Blows's request for the capital sum, they expressed astonishment that she could be willing to tear herself away from the hero's grave, and spoke of the pain which such an act on her part would cause him in the event of his being conscious of it. In order to show that they were reasonable men, they allowed her an extra shilling that week.

The hero threw the dole on the bedroom floor, and in a speech bristling with personalities, consigned the committee to perdition. The confinement was beginning to tell upon him, and two nights afterward, just before midnight, he slipped out for a breath of fresh air.

It was a clear night, and all Gravelton with one exception, appeared to have gone to bed. The exception was Police-constable Collins, and he, after tracking the skulking figure of Mr. Blows and finally bringing it to bay in a doorway, kept his for a fort-night. As a sensible man, Mr. Blows took no credit to himself for the circumstance, but a natural feeling of satisfaction at the discomfiture of a member of a force for which he had long entertained a strong objection could not be denied.

Gravelton debated this new appearance with bated breath, and even the purblind committee of the Camels had to alter their views. They no longer denied the supernatural nature of the manifestations, but, with a strange misunderstanding of Mr. Blows's desires, attributed his restlessness to dissatisfaction with the projected tombstone, and, having plenty of funds, amended their order for a plain stone at ten guineas to one in pink marble at twenty-five.

"That there committee," said Mr. Blows to his wife, in a trembling voice, as he heard of the alteration—"that there committee seem to think that they can play about with my money as they like. You go and tell 'em you won't 'ave it. And say you've given up the idea of going to Australia and you want the money to open a shop with. We'll take a little pub somewhere."

Mrs. Blows went, and returned in tears, and for two entire days her husband, a prey to gloom, sat trying to evolve fresh and original ideas for the possession of the money. On the evening of the second day he became low-spirited, and going down to the kitchen took a glass from the dresser and sat down by the beer-cask.

Almost insensibly he began to take a brighter view of things. It was Saturday night and his wife was out. He shook his head indulgently as he thought of her, and began to realise how foolish he had been to entrust such a delicate mission to a woman. The Ancient Order of Camels wanted a man to talk to them—a man who knew the world and could assail them with unanswerable arguments. Having applied every known test to make sure that the cask was empty, he took his cap from a nail and sallied out into the street.

Old Mrs. Martin, a neighbour, saw him first, and announced the fact with a scream that brought a dozen people round her. Bereft of speech, she mouthed dumbly at Mr. Blows.

"I ain't touch—touched her," said that gentleman, earnestly. "I ain't— been near 'er."

The crowd regarded him wild-eyed. Fresh members came running up, and pushing for a front place fell back hastily on the main body and watched breathlessly. Mr. Blows, disquieted by their silence, renewed his protestations.

"I was coming 'long—"

He broke off suddenly and, turning round, gazed with some heat at a gentleman who was endeavouring to ascertain whether an umbrella would pass through him. The investigator backed hastily into the crowd again, and a faint murmur of surprise arose as the indignant Mr. Blows rubbed the place.

"He's alive, I tell you," said a voice. "What cheer, Jack!"

"'Ullo, Bill," said Mr. Blows, genially.

Bill came forward cautiously, and, first shaking hands, satisfied himself by various little taps and prods that his friend was really alive.

"It's all right," he shouted; "come and feel."

At least fifty hands accepted the invitation, and, ignoring the threats and entreaties of Mr. Blows, who was a highly ticklish subject, wandered briskly over his anatomy. He broke free at last and, supported by Bill and a friend, set off for the Peal o' Bells.

By the time he arrived there his following had swollen to immense proportions. Windows were thrown up, and people standing on their doorsteps shouted inquiries. Congratulations met him on all sides, and the joy of Mr. Joseph Carter was so great that Mr. Blows was quite affected.

In high feather at the attention he was receiving, Mr. Blows pushed his way through the idlers at the door and ascended the short flight of stairs which led to the room where the members of the Ancient Order of Camels were holding their lodge. The crowd swarmed up after him.

The door was locked, but in response to his knocking it opened a couple of inches, and a gruff voice demanded his business. Then, before he could give it, the doorkeeper reeled back into the room, and Mr. Blows with a large following pushed his way in.

The president and his officers, who were sitting in state behind a long table at the end of the room, started to their feet with mingled cries of indignation and dismay at the intrusion. Mr. Blows, conscious of the strength of his position, walked up to them.

"Mr. Blows!" gasped the president.

"Ah, you didn't expec' see me," said Mr. Blows, with a scornful laugh "They're trying do me, do me out o' my lill bit o' money, Bill."

"But you ain't got no money," said his bewildered friend.

Mr. Blows turned and eyed him haughtily; then he confronted the staring president again.

"I've come for—my money," he said, impressively— "one 'under-eighty pounds."

"But look 'ere," said the scandalised Bill, tugging at his sleeve; "you ain't dead, Jack."

"You don't understan'," said Mr. Blows, impatiently. "They know wharri mean; one 'undereighty pounds. They want to buy me a tombstone, an' I don't want it. I want the money. Here, stop it! *Dye hear?*" The words were wrung from him by the action of the president, who, after eyeing him doubtfully during his remarks, suddenly prodded him with the butt-end of one of the property spears which leaned against his chair. The solidity of Mr. Blows was unmistakable, and with a sudden resumption of dignity the official seated himself and called for silence.

"I'm sorry to say there's been a bit of a mistake made," he said, slowly, "but I'm glad to say that Mr. Blows has come back to support his wife and family with the sweat of his own brow. Only a pound or two of the money so kindly subscribed has been spent, and the remainder will be handed back to the subscribers."

"Here," said the incensed Mr. Blows, "listen me."

"Take him away," said the president, with great dignity. "Clear the room. Strangers outside."

Two of the members approached Mr. Blows and, placing their hands on his shoulders, requested him to withdraw. He went at last, the centre of a dozen panting men, and becoming wedged on the narrow staircase, spoke fluently on such widely differing subjects as the rights of man and the shape of the president's nose.

He finished his remarks in the street, but, becoming aware at last of a strange lack of sympathy on the part of his audience, he shook off the arm of the faithful Mr. Carter and stalked moodily home.

A TIGER'S SKIN

The travelling sign-painter who was repainting the sign of the "Cauliflower" was enjoying a well-earned respite from his labours. On the old table under the shade of the elms mammoth sandwiches and a large slice of cheese waited in an untied handkerchief until such time as his thirst should be satisfied. At the other side of the table the oldest man in Claybury, drawing gently at a long clay pipe, turned a dim and regretful eye up at the old signboard.

"I've drunk my beer under it for pretty near seventy years," he said, with a sigh. "It's a pity it couldn't ha' lasted my time."

The painter, slowly pushing a wedge of sandwich into his mouth, regarded him indulgently.

"It's all through two young gentlemen as was passing through 'ere a month or two ago," continued the old man; "they told Smith, the landlord, they'd been looking all over the place for the 'Cauliflower,' and when Smith showed 'em the sign they said they thought it was the 'George the Fourth,' and a very good likeness, too."

The painter laughed and took another look at the old sign; then, with the nervousness of the true artist, he took a look at his own. One or two shadows—

He flung his legs over the bench and took up his brushes. In ten minutes the most fervent loyalist would have looked in vain for any resemblance, and with a sigh at the pitfalls which beset the artist he returned to his interrupted meal and hailed the house for more beer.

"There's nobody could mistake your sign for anything but a cauliflower," said the old man; "it looks good enough to eat."

The painter smiled and pushed his mug across the table. He was a tender-hearted man, and once— when painting the sign of the "Sir Wilfrid Lawson"—knew himself what it was to lack beer. He began to discourse on art, and spoke somewhat disparagingly of the cauliflower as a subject. With a shake of his head he spoke of the possibilities of a spotted cow or a blue lion.

"Talking of lions," said the ancient, musingly, "I s'pose as you never 'eard tell of the Claybury tiger? It was afore your time in these parts, I expect."

The painter admitted his ignorance, and, finding that the allusion had no reference to an inn, pulled out his pipe and prepared to listen.

"It's a while ago now," said the old man, slowly, "and the circus the tiger belonged to was going through Claybury to get to Wickham, when, just as they was passing Gill's farm, a steam-ingine they 'ad to draw some o' the vans broke down, and they 'ad to stop while the blacksmith mended it. That being so, they put up a big tent and 'ad the circus 'ere.

"I was one o' them as went, and I must say it was worth the money, though Henry Walker was disappointed at the man who put 'is 'ead in the lion's mouth. He said that the man frightened the lion first, before 'e did it.

"It was a great night for Claybury, and for about a week nothing else was talked of. All the children was playing at being lions and tigers and such-like, and young Roberts pretty near broke 'is back trying to see if he could ride horseback standing up.

"It was about two weeks after the circus 'ad gone when a strange thing 'appened: the big tiger broke loose. Bill Chambers brought the news first, 'aving read it in the newspaper while 'e was 'aving his tea. He brought out the paper and showed us, and soon after we 'eard all sorts o' tales of its doings.

"At first we thought the tiger was a long way off, and we was rather amused at it. Frederick Scott laughed 'imself silly a'most up 'ere one night thinking 'ow surprised a man would be if 'e come 'ome one night and found the tiger sitting in his armchair eating the baby. It didn't seem much of a laughing matter to me, and I said so; none of us liked it, and even Sam Jones, as 'ad got twins for the second time, said 'Shame!' But Frederick Scott was a man as would laugh at anything."

"When we 'eard that the tiger 'ad been seen within three miles of Claybury things began to look serious, and Peter Gubbins said that something ought to be done, but before we could think of anything to do something 'appened.

"We was sitting up 'ere one evening 'aving a mug o' beer and a pipe—same as I might be now if I'd got any baccy left—and talking about it, when we 'eard a shout and saw a ragged-looking tramp running toward us as 'ard as he could run. Every now and then he'd look over 'is shoulder and give a shout, and then run 'arder than afore.

"'It's the tiger!' ses Bill Chambers, and afore you could wink a'most he was inside the house, 'aving first upset Smith and a pot o' beer in the doorway.

"Before he could get up, Smith 'ad to wait till we was all in. His langwidge was awful for a man as 'ad a license to lose, and everybody shouting 'Tiger!' as they trod on 'im didn't ease 'is mind. He was inside a'most as soon as the last man, though, and in a flash he 'ad the door bolted just as the tramp flung 'imself agin it, all out of breath and sobbing 'is hardest to be let in.

"'Open the door,' he ses, banging on it.

"'Go away,' ses Smith.

"'It's the tiger,' screams the tramp; 'open the door.'

"'You go away,' ses Smith, 'you're attracting it to my place; run up the road and draw it off.'"

"Just at that moment John Biggs, the blacksmith, come in from the taproom, and as soon as he 'eard wot was the matter 'e took down Smith's gun from behind the bar and said he was going out to look after the wimmen and children.

"'Open the door,' he ses.

"He was trying to get out and the tramp outside was trying to get in, but Smith held on to that door like a Briton. Then John Biggs lost 'is temper, and he ups with the gun—Smith's own gun, mind you—and fetches 'im a bang over the 'ead with it. Smith fell down at once, and afore we could 'elp ourselves the door was open, the tramp was inside, and John Biggs was running up the road, shouting 'is hardest.

"We 'ad the door closed afore you could wink a'most, and then, while the tramp lay in a corner 'aving brandy, Mrs. Smith got a bowl of water and a sponge and knelt down bathing 'er husband's 'ead with it.

"'Did you see the tiger?' ses Bill Chambers.

"'See it?' ses the tramp, with a shiver. 'Oh, Lord!'

"He made signs for more brandy, and Henery Walker, wot was acting as landlord, without being asked, gave it to 'im.

"'It chased me for over a mile,' ses the tramp; 'my 'eart's breaking.'

"He gave a groan and fainted right off. A terrible faint it was, too, and for some time we thought 'ed never come round agin. First they poured brandy down 'is throat, then gin, and then beer, and still 'e didn't come round, but lay quiet with 'is eyes closed and a horrible smile on 'is face.

"He come round at last, and with nothing stronger than water, which Mrs. Smith kept pouring into 'is mouth. First thing we noticed was that the smile went, then 'is eyes opened, and suddenly 'e sat up with a shiver and gave such a dreadful scream that we thought at first the tiger was on top of us.

"Then 'e told us 'ow he was sitting washing 'is shirt in a ditch, when he 'eard a snuffling noise and saw the 'ead of a big tiger sticking through the hedge the other side. He left 'is shirt and ran, and 'e said that, fortunately, the tiger stopped to tear the shirt to pieces, else 'is last hour would 'ave arrived.

"When 'e 'ad finished Smith went upstairs and looked out of the bedroom winders, but 'e couldn't see any signs of the tiger, and 'e said no doubt it 'ad gone down to the village to see wot it could pick up, or p'raps it 'ad eaten John Biggs.

"However that might be, nobody cared to go outside to see, and after it got dark we liked going 'ome less than ever.

"Up to ten o'clock we did very well, and then Smith began to talk about 'is license. He said it was all rubbish being afraid to go 'ome, and that, at any rate, the tiger couldn't eat more than one of us, and while 'e was doing that there was the chance for the others to get 'ome safe. Two or three of 'em took a dislike to Smith that night and told 'im so.

"The end of it was we all slept in the tap-room that night. It seemed strange at first, but anything was better than going 'ome in the dark, and we all slept till about four next morning, when we woke up and found the tramp 'ad gone and left the front door standing wide open.

"We took a careful look-out, and by-and-by first one started off and then another to see whether their wives and children 'ad been eaten or not. Not a soul 'ad been touched, but the wimmen and children was that scared there was no doing anything with 'em. None o' the children would go to school, and they sat at 'ome all day with the front winder blocked up with a mattress to keep the tiger out.

"Nobody liked going to work, but it 'ad to be done and as Farmer Gill said that tigers went to sleep all day and only came out toward evening we was a bit comforted. Not a soul went up to the 'Cauliflower' that evening for fear of coming 'ome in the dark, but as nothing 'appened that night we began to 'ope as the tiger 'ad travelled further on.

"Bob Pretty laughed at the whole thing and said 'e didn't believe there was a tiger; but nobody minded wot 'e said, Bob Pretty being, as I've often told people, the black sheep o' Claybury, wot with poaching and, wot was worse, 'is artfulness.

"But the very next morning something 'appened that made Bob Pretty look silly and wish 'e 'adn't talked quite so fast; for at five o'clock Frederick Scott, going down to feed 'is hins, found as the tiger 'ad been there afore 'im and 'ad eaten no less than seven of 'em. The side of the hin-'ouse was all broke in, there was a few feathers lying on the ground, and two little chicks smashed and dead beside 'em.

"The way Frederick Scott went on about it you'd 'ardly believe. He said that Govinment 'ud 'ave to make it up to 'im, and instead o' going to work 'e put the two little chicks and the feathers into a pudding basin and walked to Cudford, four miles off, where they 'ad a policeman.

"He saw the policeman, William White by name, standing at the back door of the 'Fox and Hounds' public house, throwing a 'andful o' corn to the landlord's fowls, and the first thing Mr. White ses was, 'it's off my beat,' he ses.

"'But you might do it in your spare time, Mr. White,' ses Frederick Scott. It's very likely that the tiger'll come back to my hin 'ouse for the rest of 'em, and he'd be very surprised if 'e popped 'is 'ead in and see you there waiting for 'im.'

"He'd 'ave reason to be,' ses Policeman White, staring at 'im.

"'Think of the praise you'd get,' said Frederick Scott, coaxing like.

"'Look 'ere,' ses Policeman White, 'if you don't take yourself and that pudding basin off pretty quick, you'll come along o' me, d'ye see? You've been drinking and you're in a excited state.'

"He gave Frederick Scott a push and follered 'im along the road, and every time Frederick stopped to ask 'im wot 'e was doing of 'e gave 'im another push to show 'im.

"Frederick Scott told us all about it that evening, and some of the bravest of us went up to the 'Cauliflower' to talk over wot was to be done, though we took care to get 'ome while it was quite light. That night Peter Gubbins's two pigs went. They were two o' the likeliest pigs I ever seed, and all Peter Gubbins could do was to sit up in bed shivering and listening to their squeals as the tiger dragged 'em off. Pretty near all Claybury was round that sty next morning looking at the broken fence. Some of them looked for the tiger's footmarks, but it was dry weather and they couldn't see any. Nobody knew whose turn it would be next, and the most sensible man there, Sam Jones, went straight off 'ome and killed his pig afore 'e went to work.

"Nobody knew what to do; Farmer Hall said as it was a soldier's job, and 'e drove over to Wickham to tell the police so, but nothing came of it, and that night at ten minutes to twelve Bill Chambers's pig went. It was one o' the biggest pigs ever raised in Claybury, but the tiger got it off as easy as possible. Bill 'ad the bravery to look out of the winder when 'e 'eard the pig squeal, but there was such a awful snarling noise that 'e daresn't move 'and or foot.

"Dicky Weed's idea was for people with pigs and such-like to keep 'em in the house of a night, but Peter Gubbins and Bill Chambers both pointed out that the tiger could break a back door with one blow of 'is paw, and that if 'e got inside he might take something else instead o' pig. And they said that it was no worse for other people to lose pigs than wot it was for them.

"The odd thing about it was that all this time nobody 'ad ever seen the tiger except the tramp and people sent their children back to school agin and felt safe going about in the daytime till little Charlie Gubbins came running 'ome crying and saying that 'e'd seen it. Next morning a lot more children see it and was afraid to go to school, and people began to wonder wot 'ud happen when all the pigs and poultry was eaten.

"Then Henery Walker see it. We was sitting inside 'ere with scythes, and pitchforks, and such-like things handy, when we see 'im come in without 'is hat. His eyes were staring and 'is hair was all rumpled. He called for a pot o' ale and drank it nearly off, and then 'e sat gasping and 'olding the mug between 'is legs and shaking 'is 'ead at the floor till everybody 'ad left off talking to look at 'im.

"'Wot's the matter, Henery?' ses one of 'em.

"'Don't ask me,' ses Henery Walker, with a shiver.

"'You don't mean to say as 'ow you've seen the tiger?" ses Bill Chambers.

"Henery Walker didn't answer 'im. He got up and walked back'ards and for'ards, still with that frightened look in 'is eyes, and once or twice 'e give such a terrible start that 'e frightened us 'arf out of our wits. Then Bill Chambers took and forced 'im into a chair and give 'im two o' gin and patted 'im on the back, and at last Henery Walker got 'is senses back agin and told us 'ow the tiger 'ad chased 'im all round and round the trees in Plashett's Wood until 'e managed to climb up a tree and escape it. He said the tiger 'ad kept 'im there for over an hour, and then suddenly turned round and bolted off up the road to Wickham.

"It was a merciful escape, and everybody said so except Sam Jones, and 'e asked so many questions that at last Henery Walker asked 'im outright if 'e disbelieved 'is word.

"'It's all right, Sam,' ses Bob Pretty, as 'ad come in just after Henery Walker. 'I see 'im with the tiger after 'im.'

"'Wot?' ses Henery, staring at him.

"'I see it all, Henery,' ses Bob Pretty, 'and I see your pluck. It was all you could do to make up your mind to run from it. I believe if you'd 'ad a fork in your 'and you'd 'ave made a fight for it."

"Everybody said 'Bravo!'; but Henery Walker didn't seem to like it at all. He sat still, looking at Bob Pretty, and at last 'e ses, 'Where was you?' 'e s,es.

"'Up another tree, Henery, where you couldn't see me,' ses Bob Pretty, smiling at 'im.

"Henery Walker, wot was drinking some beer, choked a bit, and then 'e put the mug down and went straight off 'ome without saying a word to anybody. I knew 'e didn't like Bob Pretty, but I couldn't see why 'e should be cross about 'is speaking up for 'im as 'e had done, but Bob said as it was 'is modesty, and 'e thought more of 'im for it.

"After that things got worse than ever; the wimmen and children stayed indoors and kept the doors shut, and the men never knew when they went out to work whether they'd come 'ome agin. They used to kiss their children afore they went out of a morning, and their wives too, some of 'em; even men who'd been married for years did. And several more of 'em see the tiger while they was at work, and came running 'ome to tell about it.

"The tiger 'ad been making free with Claybury pigs and such-like for pretty near a week, and nothing 'ad been done to try and catch it, and wot made Claybury men madder than anything else was folks at Wickham saying it was all a mistake, and the tiger 'adn't escaped at all. Even parson, who'd been away for a holiday, said so, and Henery Walker told 'is wife that if she ever set foot inside the church agin 'ed ask 'is old mother to come and live with 'em.

"It was all very well for parson to talk, but the very night he come back Henery Walker's pig went, and at the same time George Kettle lost five or six ducks.

"He was a quiet man, was George, but when 'is temper was up 'e didn't care for anything. Afore he came to Claybury 'e 'ad been in the Militia, and that evening at the 'Cauliflower' 'e turned up with a gun over 'is shoulder and made a speech, and asked who was game to go with 'im and hunt the tiger. Bill Chambers, who was still grieving after 'is pig, said 'e would, then another man offered, until at last there was seventeen of 'em. Some of 'em 'ad scythes and some pitchforks, and one or two of 'em guns, and it was one o' the finest sights I ever seed when George Kettle stood 'em in rows of four and marched 'em off.

"They went straight up the road, then across Farmer Gill's fields to get to Plashett's wood, where they thought the tiger 'ud most likely be, and the nearer they got to the wood the slower they walked. The sun 'ad just gone down and the wood looked very quiet and dark, but John Biggs, the blacksmith, and George Kettle walked in first and the others follered, keeping so close together that Sam Jones 'ad a few words over his shoulder with Bill Chambers about the way 'e was carrying 'is pitchfork.

"Every now and then somebody 'ud say, *'Wot's that!'* and they'd all stop and crowd together and think the time 'ad come, but it 'adn't, and then they'd go on agin, trembling, until they'd walked all round the wood without seeing anything but one or two rabbits. John Biggs and George Kettle wanted for to stay there till it was dark, but the others wouldn't 'ear of it for fear of frightening their wives, and just as it was getting dark they all come tramp, tramp, back to the 'Cauliflower' agin.

"Smith stood 'em 'arf a pint apiece, and they was all outside 'ere fancying theirselves a bit for wot they'd done when we see old man Parsley coming along on two sticks as fast as 'e could come.

"'Are you brave lads a-looking for the tiger?' he asks.

"'Yes,' ses John Biggs.

"'Then 'urry up, for the sake of mercy,' ses old Mr. Parsley, putting 'is 'and on the table and going off into a fit of coughing; 'it's just gone into Bob Pretty's cottage. I was passing and saw it.'

"George Kettle snatches up 'is gun and shouts out to 'is men to come along. Some of 'em was for 'anging back at first, some because they didn't like the tiger and some because they didn't like Bob Pretty, but John Biggs drove 'em in front of 'im like a flock o' sheep and then they gave a cheer and ran after George Kettle, full pelt up the road.

"A few wimmen and children was at their doors as they passed, but they took fright and went indoors screaming. There was a lamp in Bob Pretty's front room, but the door was closed and the 'ouse was silent as the grave.

"George Kettle and the men with the guns went first, then came the pitchforks, and last of all the scythes. Just as George Kettle put 'is 'and on the door he 'eard something moving inside, and the next moment the door opened and there stood Bob Pretty.

"'What the dickens!' 'e ses, starting back as 'e see the guns and pitchforks pointing at 'im.

"''Ave you killed it, Bob?' ses George Kettle.

"'Killed *wot?*' ses Bob Pretty. 'Be careful o' them guns. Take your fingers off the triggers.'

"'The tiger's in your 'ouse, Bob,' ses George Kettle, in a whisper. ''Ave you on'y just come in?'

"'Look 'ere,' ses Bob Pretty. 'I don't want any o' your games. You go and play 'em somewhere else.'

"'It ain't a game,' ses John Biggs; 'the tiger's in your 'ouse and we're going to kill it. Now, then, lads.'

"They all went in in a 'eap, pushing Bob Pretty in front of 'em, till the room was full. Only one man with a scythe got in, and they wouldn't 'ave let 'im in if they'd known. It a'most made 'em forget the tiger for the time.

"George Kettle opened the door wot led into the kitchen, and then 'e sprang back with such a shout that the man with the scythe tried to escape, taking Henery Walker along with 'im. George Kettle tried to speak, but couldn't. All 'e could do was to point with 'is finger at Bob Pretty's kitchen—*and Bob Pretty's kitchen was for all the world like a pork-butcher's shop.* There was joints o' pork 'anging from the ceiling, two brine tubs as full as they could be, and quite a string of fowls and ducks all ready for market.

"'Wot d'ye mean by coming into my 'ouse?' ses Bob Pretty, blustering. 'If you don't clear out pretty quick, I'll make you.'

"Nobody answered 'im; they was all examining 'ands o' pork and fowls and such-like.

"'There's the tiger,' ses Henery Walker, pointing at Bob Pretty; 'that's wot old man Parsley meant.'

"'Somebody go and fetch Policeman White,' ses a voice.

"'I wish they would,' ses Bob Pretty. "I'll 'ave the law on you all for breaking into my 'ouse like this, see if I don't.'

"'Where'd you get all this pork from?' ses the blacksmith.

"'And them ducks and hins?' ses George Kettle.

"'That's my bisness,' ses Bob Pretty, staring 'em full in the face. 'I just 'ad a excellent oppertunity offered me of going into the pork and poultry line and I took it. Now, all them as doesn't want to buy any pork or fowls go out o' my house.'

"'You're a thief, Bob Pretty!' says Henery Walker. 'You stole it all.'

"'Take care wot you're saying, Henery,' ses Bob Pretty, 'else I'll make you prove your words.'

"'You stole my pig,' ses Herbert Smith.

"'Oh, 'ave I?' ses Bob, reaching down a 'and o' pork. 'Is that your pig?' he ses.

"'It's just about the size o' my pore pig,' ses Herbert Smith.

"'Very usual size, I call it,' ses Bob Pretty; 'and them ducks and hins very usual-looking hins and ducks, I call 'em, except that they don't grow 'em so fat in these parts. It's a fine thing when a man's doing a honest bisness to 'ave these charges brought agin 'im. Dis'eartening, I call it. I don't mind telling you that the tiger got in at my back winder the other night and took arf a pound o' sausage, but you don't 'ear me complaining and going about calling other people thieves.'

"'Tiger be hanged,' ses Henery Walker, who was almost certain that a loin o' pork on the table was off 'is pig; 'you're the only tiger in these parts.'

"Why, Henery,' ses Bob Pretty, 'wot are you a-thinkin' of? Where's your memory? Why, it's on'y two or three days ago you see it and 'ad to get up a tree out of its way.'

"He smiled and shook 'is 'ead at 'im, but Henery Walker on'y kept opening and shutting 'is mouth, and at last 'e went outside without saying a word.

"'And Sam Jones see it, too,' ses Bob Pretty; 'didn't you, Sam?'

"Sam didn't answer 'im.

"'And Charlie Hall and Jack Minns and a lot more,' ses Bob; 'besides, I see it myself. I can believe my own eyes, I s'pose?'

"'We'll have the law on you,' ses Sam Jones.

"'As you like,' ses Bob Pretty; 'but I tell you plain, I've got all the bills for this properly made out, upstairs. And there's pretty near a dozen of you as'll 'ave to go in the box and swear as you saw the tiger. Now, can I sell any of you a bit o' pork afore you go? It's delicious eating, and as soon as you taste it you'll know it wasn't grown in Claybury. Or a pair o' ducks wot 'ave come from two 'undered miles off, and yet look as fresh as if they was on'y killed last night.'

"George Kettle, whose ducks 'ad gone the night afore, went into the front room and walked up and down fighting for 'is breath, but it was all no good; nobody ever got the better o' Bob Pretty. None of 'em could swear to their property, and even when it became known a month later that Bob Pretty and the tramp knew each other, nothing was done. But nobody ever 'eard any more of the tiger from that day to this."

ADMIRAL PETERS

Mr. George Burton, naval pensioner, sat at the door of his lodgings gazing in placid content at the sea. It was early summer, and the air was heavy with the scent of flowers; Mr. Burton's pipe was cold and empty, and his pouch upstairs. He shook his head gently as he realised this, and, yielding to the drowsy quiet of his surroundings, laid aside the useless pipe and fell into a doze.

He was awakened half an hour later by the sound of footsteps. A tall, strongly built man was approaching from the direction of the town, and Mr. Burton, as he gazed at him sleepily, began to wonder where he had seen him before. Even when the stranger stopped and stood smiling down at him his memory proved unequal to the occasion, and he sat staring at the handsome, shaven face, with its little fringe of grey whisker, waiting for enlightenment.

"George, my buck," said the stranger, giving him a hearty slap on the shoulder, "how goes it?" "D—

Bless my eyes, I mean," said Mr. Burton, correcting himself, "if it ain't Joe Stiles. I didn't know you without your beard."

"That's me," said the other. "It's quite by accident I heard where you were living, George; I offered to go and sling my hammock with old Dingle for a week or two, and he told me. Nice quiet little place, Seacombe. Ah, you were lucky to get your pension, George."

"I deserved it," said Mr. Burton, sharply, as he fancied he detected something ambiguous in his friend's remark.

"Of course you did," said Mr. Stiles; "so did I, but I didn't get it. Well, it's a poor heart that never rejoices. What about that drink you were speaking of, George?"

"I hardly ever touch anything now," replied his friend.

"I was thinking about myself," said Mr. Stiles. "I can't bear the stuff, but the doctor says I must have it. You know what doctors are, George!"

Mr. Burton did not deign to reply, but led the way indoors.

"Very comfortable quarters, George," remarked Mr. Stiles, gazing round the room approvingly; "ship-shape and tidy. I'm glad I met old Dingle. Why, I might never ha' seen you again; and us such pals, too."

His host grunted, and from the back of a small cupboard, produced a bottle of whisky and a glass, and set them on the table. After a momentary hesitation he found another glass.

"Our noble selves," said Mr. Stiles, with a tinge of reproach in his tones, "and may we never forget old friendships."

Mr. Burton drank the toast. "I hardly know what it's like now, Joe," he said, slowly. "You wouldn't believe how soon you can lose the taste for it."

Mr. Stiles said he would take his word for it. "You've got some nice little public-houses about here, too," he remarked. "There's one I passed called the Cock and Flowerpot; nice cosy little place it would be to spend the evening in."

"I never go there," said Mr. Burton, hastily. "I—a friend o' mine here doesn't approve o' public-'ouses."

"What's the matter with him?" inquired his friend, anxiously.

"It's—it's a 'er," said Mr. Burton, in some confusion.

Mr. Stiles threw himself back in his chair and eyed him with amazement. Then, recovering his presence of mind, he reached out his hand for the bottle.

"We'll drink her health," he said, in a deep voice. "What's her name?"

"Mrs. Dutton," was the reply.

Mr. Stiles, with one hand on his heart, toasted her feelingly; then, filling up again, he drank to the "happy couple."

"She's very strict about drink," said Mr. Burton, eyeing these proceedings with some severity.

"Any—dibs?" inquired Mr. Stiles, slapping a pocket which failed to ring in response.

"She's comfortable," replied the other, awkwardly. "Got a little stationer's shop in the town; steady, old-fashioned business. She's chapel, and very strict."

"Just what you want," remarked Mr. Stiles, placing his glass on the table. "What d'ye say to a stroll?"

Mr. Burton assented, and, having replaced the black bottle in the cupboard, led the way along the cliffs toward the town some half-mile distant, Mr. Stiles beguiling the way by narrating his adventures since they had last met. A certain swagger and richness of deportment were explained by his statement that he had been on the stage.

"Only walking on," he said, with a shake of his head. "The only speaking part I ever had was a cough. You ought to ha' heard that cough, George!"

Mr. Burton politely voiced his regrets and watched him anxiously. Mr. Stiles, shaking his head over a somewhat unsuccessful career, was making a bee-line for the Cock and Flowerpot.

"Just for a small soda," he explained, and, once inside, changed his mind and had whisky instead. Mr. Burton, sacrificing principle to friendship, had one with him. The bar more than fulfilled Mr. Stiles's ideas as to its cosiness, and within the space of ten minutes he was on excellent terms with the regular clients. Into the little, old-world bar, with its loud-ticking clock, its Windsor-chairs, and its cracked jug full of roses, he brought a breath of the bustle of the great city and tales of the great cities beyond the seas. Refreshment was forced upon him, and Mr. Burton, pleased at his friend's success, shared mildly in his reception. It was nine o'clock before they departed, and then they only left to please the landlord.

"Nice lot o' chaps," said Mr. Stiles, as he stumbled out into the sweet, cool air. "Catch hold—o' my—arm, George. Brace me—up a bit."

Mr. Burton complied, and his friend, reassured as to his footing, burst into song. In a stentorian voice he sang the latest song from comic opera, and then with an adjuration to Mr. Burton to see what he was about, and not to let him trip, he began, in a lumbering fashion, to dance.

Mr. Burton, still propping him up, trod a measure with fewer steps, and cast uneasy glances up the lonely road. On their left the sea broke quietly on the beach below; on their right were one or two scattered cottages, at the doors of which an occasional figure appeared to gaze in mute astonishment at the proceedings.

"Dance, George," said Mr. Stiles, who found his friend rather an encumbrance.

"Hs'h! Stop!" cried the frantic Mr. Burton, as he caught sight of a woman's figure bidding farewell in a lighted doorway.

Mr. Stiles replied with a stentorian roar, and Mr. Burton, clinging despairingly to his jigging friend lest a worse thing should happen, cast an imploring glance at Mrs. Dutton as they danced by. The evening was still light enough for him to see her face, and he piloted the corybantic Mr. Stiles the rest of the way home in a mood which accorded but ill with his steps.

His manner at breakfast next morning was so offensive that Mr. Stiles, who had risen fresh as a daisy and been out to inhale the air on the cliffs, was somewhat offended.

"You go down and see her," he said, anxiously. "Don't lose a moment; and explain to her that it was the sea-air acting on an old sunstroke."

"She ain't a fool," said Mr. Burton, gloomily.

He finished his breakfast in silence, and, leaving the repentant Mr. Stiles sitting in the doorway with a pipe, went down to the widow's to make the best explanation he could think of on the way. Mrs. Dutton's fresh-coloured face changed as he entered the shop, and her still good eyes regarded him with scornful interrogation.

"I—saw you last night," began Mr. Burton, timidly.

"I saw you, too," said Mrs. Dutton. "I couldn't believe my eyesight at first."

"It was an old shipmate of mine," said Mr. Burton. "He hadn't seen me for years, and I suppose the sight of me upset 'im."

"I dare say," replied the widow; "that and the Cock and Flowerpot, too. I heard about it."

"He would go," said the unfortunate.

"You needn't have gone," was the reply.

"I 'ad to," said Mr. Burton, with a gulp; "he—he's an old officer o' mine, and it wouldn't ha' been discipline for me to refuse."

"Officer?" repeated Mrs. Dutton.

"My old admiral," said Mr. Burton, with a gulp that nearly choked him. "You've heard me speak of Admiral Peters?"

"Admiral?" gasped the astonished widow.

"What, a-carrying on like that?"

"He's a reg'lar old sea-dog," said Mr. Burton. "He's staying with me, but of course 'e don't want it known who he is. I couldn't refuse to 'ave a drink with 'im. I was under orders, so to speak."

"No, I suppose not," said Mrs. Dutton, softening. "Fancy him staying with you!"

"He just run down for the night, but I expect he'll be going 'ome in an hour or two," said Mr. Burton, who saw an excellent reason now for hastening his guest's departure.

Mrs. Dutton's face fell. "Dear me," she murmured, "I should have liked to have seen him; you have told me so much about him. If he doesn't go quite so soon, and you would like to bring him here when you come to-night, I'm sure I should be very pleased."

"I'll mention it to 'im," said Mr. Burton, marvelling at the change in her manner.

"Didn't you say once that he was uncle to Lord Buckfast?" inquired Mrs. Dutton, casually.

"Yes," said Mr. Burton, with unnecessary doggedness; "I did."

"The idea of an admiral staying with you!" said Mrs. Dutton.

"Reg'lar old sea-dog," said Mr. Burton again; "and, besides, he don't want it known. It's a secret between us three, Mrs. Dutton."

"To be sure," said the widow. "You can tell the admiral that I shall not mention it to a soul," she added, mincingly.

Mr. Burton thanked her and withdrew, lest Mr. Stiles should follow him up before apprised of his sudden promotion. He found that gentleman, however, still sitting at the front door, smoking serenely.

"I'll stay with you for a week or two," said Mr. Stiles, briskly, as soon as the other had told his story. "It'll do you a world o' good to be seen on friendly terms with an admiral, and I'll put in a good word for you."

Mr. Burton shook his head. "No, she might find out," he said, slowly. "I think that the best thing is for you to go home after dinner, Joe, and just give 'er a look in on the way, p'r'aps. You could say a lot o' things about me in 'arf an hour."

"No, George," said Mr. Stiles, beaming on him kindly; "when I put my hand to the plough I don't draw back. It's a good speaking part, too, an admiral's. I wonder whether I might use old Peters's language."

"Certainly not," said Mr. Burton, in alarm.

"You don't know how particular she is."

Mr. Stiles sighed, and said that he would do the best he could without it. He spent most of the day on the beach smoking, and when evening came shaved himself with extreme care and brushed his serge suit with great perseverance in preparation for his visit.

Mr. Burton performed the ceremony of introduction with some awkwardness; Mr. Stiles was affecting a stateliness of manner which was not without distinction; and Mrs. Dutton, in a black silk dress and the cameo brooch which had belonged to her mother, was no less important. Mr. Burton had an odd feeling of inferiority.

"It's a very small place to ask you to, Admiral Peters," said the widow, offering him a chair.

"It's comfortable, ma'am," said Mr. Stiles, looking round approvingly. "Ah, you should see some of the palaces I've been in abroad; all show and no comfort. Not a decent chair in the place. And, as for the antimacassars—"

"Are you making a long stay, Admiral Peters?" inquired the delighted widow.

"It depends," was the reply. "My intention was just to pay a flying visit to my honest old friend Burton here—best man in my squadron—but he is so hospitable, he's been pressing me to stay for a few weeks."

"But the admiral says he must get back to-morrow morning," interposed Mr. Burton, firmly.

"Unless I have a letter at breakfast-time, Burton," said Mr. Stiles, serenely.

Mr. Burton favoured him with a mutinous scowl.

"Oh, I do hope you will," said Mrs. Dutton.

"I have a feeling that I shall," said Mr. Stiles, crossing glances with his friend. "The only thing is my people; they want me to join them at Lord Tufton's place."

Mrs. Dutton trembled with delight at being in the company of a man with such friends. "What a change shore-life must be to you after the perils of the sea!" she murmured.

"Ah!" said Mr. Stiles. "True! True!"

"The dreadful fighting," said Mrs. Dutton, closing her eyes and shuddering.

"You get used to it," said the hero, simply. "Hottest time I had I think was at the bombardment of Alexandria. I stood alone. All the men who hadn't been shot down had fled, and the shells were bursting round me like—like fireworks."

The widow clasped her hands and shuddered again.

"I was standing just behind 'im, waiting any orders he might give," said Mr. Burton.

"Were you?" said Mr. Stiles, sharply—"were you? I don't remember it, Burton."

"Why," said Mr. Burton, with a faint laugh, "I was just behind you, sir. If you remember, sir, I said to you that it was pretty hot work."

Mr. Stiles affected to consider. "No, Burton," he said, bluffly—"no; so far as my memory goes I was the only man there."

"A bit of a shell knocked my cap off, sir," persisted Mr. Burton, making laudable efforts to keep his temper.

"That'll do, my man," said the other, sharply; "not another word. You forget yourself."

He turned to the widow and began to chat about "his people" again to divert her attention from Mr. Burton, who seemed likely to cause unpleasantness by either bursting a blood-vessel or falling into a fit.

"My people have heard of Burton," he said, with a slight glance to see how that injured gentleman was progressing. "He has often shared my dangers. We have been in many tight places together. Do you remember those two nights when we were hidden in the chimney at the palace of the Sultan of Zanzibar, Burton?"

"I should think I do," said Mr. Burton, recovering somewhat.

"Stuck so tight we could hardly breathe," continued the other.

"I shall never forget it as long as I live," said Mr. Burton, who thought that the other was trying to make amends for his recent indiscretion.

"Oh, do tell me about it, Admiral Peters," cried Mrs. Dutton.

"Surely Burton has told you that?" said Mr. Stiles.

"Never breathed a word of it," said the widow, gazing somewhat reproachfully at the discomfited Mr. Burton.

"Well, tell it now, Burton," said Mr. Stiles.

"You tell it better than I do, sir," said the other.

"No, no," said Mr. Stiles, whose powers of invention were not always to be relied upon. "You tell it; it's your story."

The widow looked from one to the other. "It's your story, sir," said Mr. Burton.

"No, I won't tell it," said Mr. Stiles. "It wouldn't be fair to you, Burton. I'd forgotten that when I spoke. Of course, you were young at the time, still—"

"I done nothing that I'm ashamed of, sir," said Mr. Burton, trembling with passion.

"I think it's very hard if I'm not to hear it," said Mrs. Dutton, with her most fascinating air.

Mr. Stiles gave her a significant glance, and screwing up his lips nodded in the direction of Mr. Burton.

"At any rate, you were in the chimney with me, sir," said that unfortunate.

"Ah!" said the other, severely. "But what was I there for, my man?"

Mr. Burton could not tell him; he could only stare at him in a frenzy of passion and dismay.

"What were you there for, Admiral Peters?" inquired Mrs. Dutton.

"I was there, ma'am," said the unspeakable Mr. Stiles, slowly—"I was there to save the life of Burton. I never deserted my men—never. Whatever scrapes they got into I always did my best to get them out. News was brought to me that Burton was suffocating in the chimney of the Sultan's favourite wife, and I—"

"Sultan's favourite wife!" gasped Mrs. Dutton, staring hard at Mr. Burton, who had collapsed in his chair and was regarding the ingenious Mr. Stiles with open-mouthed stupefaction. "Good gracious!

I—I never heard of such a thing. I am surprised!"

"So am I," said Mr. Burton, thickly. "I—I—"

"How did you escape, Admiral Peters?" inquired the widow, turning from the flighty Burton in indignation.

Mr. Stiles shook his head. "To tell you that would be to bring the French Consul into it," he said, gently. "I oughtn't to have mentioned the subject at all. Burton had the good sense not to."

The widow murmured acquiescence, and stole a look at the prosaic figure of the latter gentleman which was full of scornful curiosity. With some diffidence she invited the admiral to stay to supper, and was obviously delighted when he accepted.

In the character of admiral Mr. Stiles enjoyed himself amazingly, his one regret being that no discriminating theatrical manager was present to witness his performance. His dignity increased as the evening wore on, and from good-natured patronage of the unfortunate Burton he progressed gradually until he was shouting at him. Once, when he had occasion to ask Mr. Burton if he intended to contradict him, his appearance was so terrible that his hostess turned pale and trembled with excitement.

Mr. Burton adopted the air for his own use as soon as they were clear of Mrs. Dutton's doorstep, and in good round terms demanded of Mr. Stiles what he meant by it.

"It was a difficult part to play, George," responded his friend. "We ought to have rehearsed it a bit. I did the best I could."

"Best you could?" stormed Mr. Burton. "Telling lies and ordering me about?"

"I had to play the part without any preparation, George," said the other, firmly. "You got yourself into the difficulty by saying that I was the admiral in the first place. I'll do better next time we go."

Mr. Burton, with a nasty scowl, said that there was not going to be any next time, but Mr. Stiles smiled as one having superior information. Deaf first to hints and then to requests to seek his pleasure elsewhere, he stayed on, and Mr. Burton was soon brought to realise the difficulties which beset the path of the untruthful.

The very next visit introduced a fresh complication, it being evident to the most indifferent spectator that Mr. Stiles and the widow were getting on very friendly terms. Glances of unmistakable tenderness passed between them, and on the occasion of the third visit Mr. Burton sat an amazed and scandalised spectator of a flirtation of the most pronounced description. A despairing attempt on his part to lead the conversation into safer and, to his mind, more becoming channels only increased his discomfiture. Neither of them took any notice of it, and a minute later Mr. Stiles called the widow a "saucy little baggage," and said that she reminded him of the Duchess of Marford.

"I used to think she was the most charming woman in England," he said, meaningly.

Mrs. Dutton simpered and looked down; Mr. Stiles moved his chair a little closer to her, and then glanced thoughtfully at his friend.

"Burton," he said.

"Sir," snapped the other.

"Run back and fetch my pipe for me," said Mr. Stiles. "I left it on the mantelpiece."

Mr. Burton hesitated, and, the widow happening to look away, shook his fist at his superior officer.

"Look sharp," said Mr. Stiles, in a peremptory voice.

"I'm very sorry, sir," said Mr. Burton, whose wits were being sharpened by misfortune, "but I broke it."

"Broke it?" repeated the other.

"Yes, sir," said Mr. Burton. "I knocked it on the floor and trod on it by accident; smashed it to powder."

Mr. Stiles rated him roundly for his carelessness, and asked him whether he knew that it was a present from the Italian Ambassador.

"Burton was always a clumsy man," he said, turning to the widow. "He had the name for it when he was on the *Destruction* with me; 'Bungling Burton' they called him."

He divided the rest of the evening between flirting and recounting various anecdotes of Mr. Burton, none of which were at all flattering either to his intelligence or to his sobriety, and the victim, after one or two futile attempts at contradiction, sat in helpless wrath as he saw the infatuation of the widow. They were barely clear of the house before his pent-up emotions fell in an avalanche of words on the faithless Mr. Stiles.

"I can't help being good-looking," said the latter, with a smirk.

"Your good looks wouldn't hurt anybody," said Mr. Burton, in a grating voice; "it's the admiral business that fetches her. It's turned 'er head."

Mr. Stiles smiled. "She'll say 'snap' to my 'snip' any time," he remarked. "And remember, George, there'll always be a knife and fork laid for you when you like to come."

"I dessay," retorted Mr. Burton, with a dreadful sneer. "Only as it happens I'm going to tell 'er the truth about you first thing to-morrow morning. If I can't have 'er you sha'n't."

"That'll spoil your chance, too," said Mr. Stiles. "She'd never forgive you for fooling her like that. It seems a pity neither of us should get her."

"You're a sarpent," exclaimed Mr. Burton, savagely—"a sarpent that I've warmed in my bosom and—"

"There's no call to be indelicate, George," said Mr. Stiles, reprovingly, as he paused at the door of the house. "Let's sit down and talk it over quietly."

Mr. Burton followed him into the room and, taking a chair, waited.

"It's evident she's struck with me," said Mr. Stiles, slowly; "it's also evident that if you tell her the truth it might spoil my chances. I don't say it would, but it might. That being so, I'm agreeable to going back without seeing her again by the six-forty train to-morrow morning if it's made worth my while."

"Made worth your while?" repeated the other.

"Certainly," said the unblushing Mr. Stiles. "She's not a bad-looking woman—for her age—and it's a snug little business."

Mr. Burton, suppressing his choler, affected to ponder. "If 'arf a sovereign—" he said, at last.

"Half a fiddlestick!" said the other, impatiently. "I want ten pounds. You've just drawn your pension, and, besides, you've been a saving man all your life."

"Ten pounds?" gasped the other. "D'ye think I've got a gold-mine in the back garden?"

Mr. Stiles leaned back in his chair and crossed his feet. "I don't go for a penny less," he said, firmly. "Ten pounds and my ticket back. If you call me any more o' those names I'll make it twelve."

"And what am I to explain to Mrs. Dutton?" demanded Mr. Burton, after a quarter of an hour's altercation.

"Anything you like," said his generous friend. "Tell her I'm engaged to my cousin, and our marriage keeps being put off and off on account of my eccentric behaviour. And you can say that that was caused by a splinter of a shell striking my head. Tell any lies you like; I shall never turn up again to contradict them. If she tries to find out things about the admiral, remind her that she promised to keep his visit here secret."

For over an hour Mr. Burton sat weighing the advantages and disadvantages of this proposal, and then—Mr. Stiles refusing to seal the bargain without—shook hands upon it and went off to bed in a state of mind hovering between homicide and lunacy.

He was up in good time next morning, and, returning the shortest possible answers to the remarks of Mr. Stiles, who was in excellent feather, went with him to the railway station to be certain of his departure.

It was a delightful morning, cool and bright, and, despite his misfortunes. Mr. Burton's spirits began to rise as he thought of his approaching deliverance. Gloom again overtook him at the booking-office, where the unconscionable Mr. Stiles insisted firmly upon a first-class ticket.

"Who ever heard of an admiral riding third?" he demanded, indignantly.

"But they don't know you're an admiral," urged Mr. Burton, trying to humour him.

"No; but I feel like one," said Mr. Stiles, slapping his pocket. "I've always felt curious to see what it feels like travelling first-class; besides, you can tell Mrs. Dutton."

"I could tell 'er that in any case," returned Mr. Burton.

Mr. Stiles looked shocked, and, time pressing, Mr. Burton, breathing so hard that it impeded his utterance, purchased a first-class ticket and conducted him to the carriage. Mr. Stiles took a seat by the window and lolling back put his foot up on the cushions opposite. A large bell rang and the carriage-doors were slammed.

"Good-bye, George," said the traveller, putting his head to the window. "I've enjoyed my visit very much."

"Good riddance," said Mr. Burton, savagely.

Mr. Stiles shook his head. "I'm letting you off easy," he said, slowly. "If it hadn't ha' been for one little thing I'd have had the widow myself."

"What little thing?" demanded the other, as the train began to glide slowly out.

"My wife," said Mr. Stiles, as a huge smile spread slowly over his face. "Good-bye, George, and don't forget to give my love when you go round."

AFTER THE INQUEST

It was a still fair evening in late summer in the parish of Wapping. The hands had long since left, and the night watchman having abandoned his trust in favour of a neighbouring bar, the wharf was deserted.

An elderly seaman came to the gate and paused irresolute, then, seeing all was quiet, stole cautiously on to the jetty, and stood for some time gazing curiously down on to the deck of the billy-boy PSYCHE lying alongside.

With the exception of the mate, who, since the lamented disappearance of its late master and owner, was acting as captain, the deck was as deserted as the wharf. He was smoking an evening pipe in all the pride of a first command, his eye roving fondly from the blunt bows and untidy deck of his craft to her clumsy stern, when a slight cough from the man above attracted his attention.

"How do, George?" said the man on the jetty, somewhat sheepishly, as the other looked up.

The mate opened his mouth, and his pipe fell from it and smashed to pieces unnoticed.

"Got much stuff in her this trip?" continued the man, with an obvious attempt to appear at ease.

"The mate, still looking up, backed slowly to the other side of the deck, but made no reply.

"What's the matter, man?" said the other testily. "You don't seem overpleased to see me."

He leaned over as he spoke, and, laying hold of the rigging, descended to the deck, while the mate took his breath in short, exhilarating gasps.

"Here I am, George," said the intruder, "turned up like a bad penny, an' glad to see your handsome face again, I can tell you."

In response to this flattering remark George gurgled.

"Why," said the other, with an uneasy laugh, "did you think I was dead, George? Ha, ha! Feel that!"

He fetched the horrified man a thump in the back, which stopped even his gurgles.

"That feel like a dead man?" asked the smiter, raising his hand again. "Feel"—

The mate moved back hastily. "That'll do," said he fiercely; "ghost or no ghost, don't you hit me like that again."

"A' right, George," said the other, as he meditatively felt the stiff grey whiskers which framed his red face. "What's the news?"

"The news," said George, who was of slow habits and speech, "is that you was found last Tuesday week off St. Katherine's Stairs, you was sat on a Friday week at the Town o' Ramsgate public-house, and buried on Monday afternoon at Lowestoft."

"Buried?" gasped the other, "sat on? You've been drinking, George."

"An' a pretty penny your funeral cost, I can tell you," continued the mate. "There's a headstone being made now—'Lived lamented and died respected,' I think it is, with 'Not lost, but gone before,' at the bottom."

"Lived respected and died lamented, you mean," growled the old man; "well, a nice muddle you have made of it between you. Things always go wrong when I'm not here to look after them."

"You ain't dead, then?" said the mate, taking no notice of this unreasonable remark, "Where've you been all this long time?"

"No more than you're master o' this 'ere ship," replied Mr. Harbolt grimly. "I—I've been a bit queer in the stomach, an' I took a little drink to correct it. Foolish like, I took the wrong drink, and it must have got into my head."

"That's the worst of not being used to it," said the mate, without moving a muscle.

The skipper eyed him solemnly, but the mate stood firm.

"Arter that," continued the skipper, still watching him suspiciously, "I remember no more distinctly until this morning, when I found myself sitting on a step down Poplar way and shiverin', with the morning newspaper and a crowd round me."

"Morning newspaper!" repeated the mystified mate. "What was that for?"

"Decency. I was wrapped up in it," replied the skipper. "Where I came from or how I got there I don't know more than Adam. I s'pose I must have been ill; I seem to remember taking something out of a bottle pretty often. Some old gentleman in the crowd took me into a shop and bought me these clothes, an' here I am. My own clo'es and thirty pounds o' freight money I had in my pocket is all gone."

"Well, I'm hearty glad to see you back," said the mate. "It's quite a home-coming for you, too. Your missis is down aft."

"My missis? What the devil's she aboard for?" growled the skipper, successfully controlling his natural gratification at the news.

"She's been with us these last two trips," replied the mate. "She's had business to settle in London, and she's been going through your lockers to clear up, like."

"My lockers!" groaned the skipper. "Good heavens! there's things in them lockers I wouldn't have her see for the world; women are so fussy an' so fond o' making something out o' nothing. There's a pore female touched a bit in the upper storey, what's been writing love letters to me, George."

"Three pore females," said the precise mate; "the missis has got all the letters tied up with blue ribbon. Very far gone they was, too, poor creeters."

"George," said the skipper in a broken voice, "I'm a ruined man. I'll never hear the end o' this. I guess I'll go an' sleep for'ard this voyage, and lie low. Be keerful you don't let on I'm aboard, an' after she's home I'll take the ship again, and let the thing leak out gradual. Come to life bit by bit, so to speak. It wouldn't do to scare her, George, an' in the meantime I'll try an' think o' some explanation to tell her. You might be thinking too."

"I'll do what I can," said the mate.

"Crack me up to the old girl all you can; tell her I used to write to all sorts o' people when I got a drop of drink in me; say how thoughtful I always was of her. You might tell her about that gold locket I bought for her an' got robbed of."

"Gold locket?" said the mate in tones of great surprise. "What gold locket? Fust I've heard of it."

"Any gold locket," said the skipper irritably; "anything you can think of; you needn't be pertikler. Arter that you can drop little hints about people being buried in mistake for others, so as to prepare her a bit—I don't want to scare her."

"Leave it to me," said the mate.

"I'll go an' turn in now, I'm dead tired," said the skipper. "I s'pose Joe and the boy's asleep?"

George nodded, and meditatively watched the other as he pushed back the fore-scuttle and drew it after him as he descended. Then a thought struck the mate, and he ran hastily forward and threw his weight on the scuttle just in time to frustrate the efforts of Joe and the boy, who were coming on deck to tell him a new ghost story. The confusion below was frightful, the skipper's cry of "It's only me, Joe," not possessing the soothing effect which he intended. They calmed down at length, after their visitor had convinced them that he really was flesh and blood and fists, and the boy's attention being directed to a small rug in the corner of the foc's'le, the skipper took his bunk and was soon fast asleep.

He slept so soundly that the noise of the vessel getting under way failed to rouse him, and she was well out in the open river when he awoke, and after cautiously protruding his head through the scuttle, ventured on deck. For some time he stood eagerly sniffing the cool, sweet air, and then, after a look round, gingerly approached the mate, who was at the helm.

"Give me a hold on her," said he.

"You had better get below again, if you don't want the missis to see you," said the mate. "She's gettin' up—nasty temper she's in too."

The skipper went forward grumbling. "Send down a good breakfast, George," said he.

To his great discomfort the mate suddenly gave a low whistle, and regarded him with a look of blank dismay.

"Good gracious!" he cried, "I forgot all about it. Here's a pretty kettle of fish—well, well."

"Forgot about what?" asked the skipper uneasily.

"The crew take their meals in the cabin now," replied the mate, "'cos the missis says it's more cheerful for 'em, and she's l'arning 'em to eat their wittles properly."

The skipper looked at him aghast. "You'll have to smuggle me up some grub," he said at length. "I'm not going to starve for nobody."

"Easier said than done," said the mate. "The missis has got eyes like needles; still, I'll do the best I can for you. Look out! Here she comes."

The skipper fled hastily, and, safe down below, explained to the crew how they were to secrete portions of their breakfast for his benefit. The amount of explanation required for so simple a matter was remarkable, the crew manifesting a denseness which irritated him almost beyond endurance. They promised, however, to do the best they could for him, and returned in triumph after a hearty meal, and presented their enraged commander with a few greasy crumbs and the tail of a bloater.

For the next two days the wind was against them, and they made but little progress. Mrs. Harbolt spent most of her time on deck, thereby confining her husband to his evil-smelling quarters below. Matters were not improved for him by his treatment of the crew, who, resenting his rough treatment of them, were doing their best to starve him into civility. Most of the time he kept in his bunk—or rather Jemmy's bunk—a prey to despondency and hunger of an acute type, venturing on deck only at night to prowl uneasily about and bemoan his condition.

On the third night Mrs. Harbolt was later in retiring than usual, and it was nearly midnight before the skipper, who had been indignantly waiting for her to go, was able to get on deck and hold counsel with the mate.

"I've done what I could for you," said the latter, fishing a crust from his pocket, which Harbolt took thankfully. "I've told her all the yarns I could think of about people turning up after they was buried and the like."

"What'd she say?" queried the skipper eagerly, between his bites.

"Told me not to talk like that," said the mate; "said it showed a want o' trust in Providence to hint at such things. Then I told her what you asked me about the locket, only I made it a bracelet worth ten pounds."

"That pleased her?" suggested the other hopefully.

The mate shook his head. "She said I was a born fool to believe you'd been robbed of it," he replied. "She said what you'd done was to give it to one o' them pore females. She's been going on frightful about it all the afternoon—won't talk o' nothing else."

"I don't know what's to be done," groaned the skipper despondently. "I shall be dead afore we get to port this wind holds. Go down and get me something to eat George; I'm starving."

"Everything's locked up, as I told you afore," said the mate.

"As the master of this ship," said the skipper, drawing himself up, "I order you to go down and get me something to eat. You can tell the missus it's for you if she says anything."

"I'm hanged if I will," said the mate sturdily. "Why don't you go down and have it out with her like a man? She can't eat you."

"I'm not going to," said the other shortly. "I'm a determined man, and when I say a thing I mean it. It's going to be broken to her gradual, as I said; I don't want her to be scared, poor thing."

"I know who'd be scared the most," murmured the mate.

The skipper looked at him fiercely, and then sat down wearily on the hatches with his hands between his knees, rising, after a time, to get the dipper and drink copiously from the water-cask. Then, replacing it with a sigh, he bade the mate a surly good-night and went below.

To his dismay he found when he awoke in the morning that what little wind there was had dropped in the night, and the billy-boy was just rising and falling lazily on the water in a fashion most objectionable to an empty stomach. It was the last straw, and he made things so uncomfortable below that the crew were glad to escape on deck, where they squatted down in the bows, and proceeded to review a situation which was rapidly becoming unbearable.

"I've 'ad enough of it, Joe," grumbled the boy. "I'm sore all over with sleeping on the floor, and the old man's temper gets wuss and wuss. I'm going to be ill."

"Whaffor?" queried Joe dully.

"You tell the missus I'm down below ill. Say you think I'm dying," responded the infant Machiavelli, "then you'll see somethink if you keep your eyes open."

He went below again, not without a little nervousness, and, clambering into Joe's bunk, rolled over on his back and gave a deep groan.

"What's the matter with YOU!" growled the skipper, who was lying in the other bunk staving off the pangs of hunger with a pipe.

"I'm very ill—dying," said Jemmy, with another groan.

"You'd better stay in bed and have your breakfast brought down here, then," said the skipper kindly.

"I don't want no breakfast," said Jem faintly.

"That's no reason why you shouldn't have it sent down, you unfeeling little brute," said the skipper indignantly. "You tell Joe to bring you down a great plate o' cold meat and pickles, and some coffee; that's what you want."

"All right, sir," said Jemmy. "I hope they won't let the missus come down here, in case it's something catching. I wouldn't like her to be took bad."

"Eh?" said the skipper, in alarm. "Certainly not. Here, you go up and die on deck. Hurry up with you."

"I can't; I'm too weak," said Jemmy.

"You get up on deck at once; d'ye hear me?" hissed the skipper, in alarm.

"I c-c-c-can't help it," sobbed Jemmy, who was enjoying the situation amazingly. "I b'lieve it's sleeping on the hard floor's snapped something inside me."

"If you don't go I'll take you," said the skipper, and he was about to rise to put his threat into execution when a shadow fell across the opening, and a voice, which thrilled him to the core, said softly, "Jemmy!"

"Yes 'm?" said Jemmy languidly, as the skipper flattened himself in his bunk and drew the clothes over him.

"How do you feel?" inquired Mrs. Harbolt.

"Bad all over," said Jemmy. "Oh, don't come down, mum—please don't."

"Rubbish!" said Mrs. Harbolt tartly, as she came slowly and carefully down backwards. "What a dark hole this is, Jemmy. No wonder you're ill. Put your tongue out."

Jemmy complied.

"I can't see properly here," murmured the lady, "but it looks very large. S'pose you go in the other bunk, Jemmy. It's a good bit higher than this, and you'd get more air and be more comfortable altogether."

"Joe wouldn't like it, mum," said the boy anxiously. The last glimpse he had had of the skipper's face did not make him yearn to share his bed with him.

"Stuff an' nonsense!" said Mrs. Harbolt hotly. "Who's Joe, I'd like to know? Out you come."

"I can't move, mum," said Jemmy firmly.

"Nonsense!" said the lady. "I'll just put it straight for you first, then in it you go."

"No, don't, mum," shouted Jemmy, now thoroughly alarmed at the success of his plot. "There, there's a gentleman in that bunk. A gentleman we brought from London for a change of sea air."

"My goodness gracious!" ejaculated the surprised Mrs. Harbolt. "I never did. Why, what's he had to eat?"

"He—he—didn't want nothing to eat," said Jemmy, with a woeful disregard for facts.

"What's the matter with him?" inquired Mrs. Harbolt, eyeing the bunk curiously. "What's his name? Who is he?"

"He's been lost a long time," said Jemmy, "and he's forgotten who he is—he's a oldish man with a red face an' a little white whisker all round it—a very nice-looking man, I mean," he interposed hurriedly. "I don't think he's quite right in his head, 'cos he says he ought to have been buried instead of someone else. Oh!"

The last word was almost a scream, for Mrs. Harbolt, staggering back, pinched him convulsively.

"Jemmy!" she gasped, in a trembling voice, as she suddenly remembered certain mysterious hints thrown out by the mate. "Who is it?"

"The CAPTAIN!" said Jemmy, and, breaking from her clasp, slipped from his bed and darted hastily on deck, just as the pallid face of his commander broke through the blankets and beamed anxiously on his wife.

Five minutes later, as the crew gathered aft were curiously eyeing the foc's'le, Mrs. Harbolt and the skipper came on deck. To the great astonishment of the mate, the eyes of the redoubtable woman were slightly wet, and, regardless of the presence of the men, she clung fondly to her husband as they walked slowly to the cabin. Ere they went below, however, she called the grinning Jemmy to her, and, to his private grief and public shame, tucked his head under her arm and kissed him fondly.

ALF'S DREAM

"I've just been drinking a man's health," said the night watchman, coming slowly on to the wharf and wiping his mouth with the back of his hand; "he's come in for a matter of three 'undred and twenty pounds, and he stood me arf a pint—arf a pint!"

He dragged a small empty towards him, and after planing the surface with his hand sat down and gazed scornfully across the river.

"Four ale," he said, with a hard laugh; "and when I asked 'im—just for the look of the thing, and to give 'im a hint—whether he'd 'ave another, he said 'yes.'"

The night watchman rose and paced restlessly up and down the jetty.

"Money," he said, at last, resuming his wonted calm and lowering himself carefully to the box again—"money always gets left to the wrong people; some of the kindest-'arted men I've ever known 'ave never had a ha'penny left 'em, while teetotaler arter teetotaler wot I've heard of 'ave come in for fortins."

It's 'ard lines though, sometimes, waiting for other people's money. I knew o' one chap that waited over forty years for 'is grandmother to die and leave 'im her money; and she died of catching cold at 'is funeral. Another chap I knew, arter waiting years and years for 'is rich aunt to die, was hung because she committed suicide.

It's always risky work waiting for other people to die and leave you money. Sometimes they don't die; sometimes they marry agin; and sometimes they leave it to other people instead.

Talking of marrying agin reminds me o' something that 'appened to a young fellow I knew named Alf Simms. Being an orphan 'e was brought up by his uncle, George Hatchard, a widowed man of about sixty. Alf used to go to sea off and on, but more off than on, his uncle 'aving quite a tidy bit of 'ouse property, and it being understood that Alf was to have it arter he 'ad gone. His uncle used to like to 'ave him at 'ome, and Alf didn't like work, so it suited both parties.

I used to give Alf a bit of advice sometimes, sixty being a dangerous age for a man, especially when he 'as been a widower for so long he 'as had time to forget wot being married's like; but I must do Alf the credit to say it wasn't wanted. He 'ad got a very old 'ead on his shoulders, and always picked the housekeeper 'imself to save the old man the trouble. I saw two of 'em, and I dare say I could 'ave seen more, only I didn't want to.

Cleverness is a good thing in its way, but there's such a thing as being too clever, and the last 'ousekeeper young Alf picked died of old age a week arter he 'ad gone to sea. She passed away while she was drawing George Hatchard's supper beer, and he lost ten gallons o' the best bitter ale and his 'ousekeeper at the same time.

It was four months arter that afore Alf came 'ome, and the fust sight of the new 'ousekeeper, wot opened the door to 'im, upset 'im terrible. She was the right side o' sixty to begin with, and only ordinary plain. Then she was as clean as a new pin, and dressed up as though she was going out to tea.

"Oh, you're Alfred, I s'pose?" she ses, looking at 'im.

"Mr. Simms is my name," ses young Alf, starting and drawing hisself up.

"I know you by your portrait," ses the 'ousekeeper. "Come in. 'Ave you 'ad a pleasant v'y'ge? Wipe your boots."

Alfred wiped 'is boots afore he thought of wot he was doing. Then he drew hisself up stiff agin and marched into the parlor.

"Sit down," ses the 'ousekeeper, in a kind voice.

Alfred sat down afore he thought wot 'e was doing agin.

"I always like to see people comfortable," ses the 'ousekeeper; "it's my way. It's warm weather for the time o' year, ain't it? George is upstairs, but he'll be down in a minute."

"Who?" ses Alf, hardly able to believe his ears.

"George," ses the 'ousekeeper.

"George? George who?" ses Alfred, very severe.

"Why your uncle, of course," ses the 'ousekeeper. "Do you think I've got a houseful of Georges?"

Young Alf sat staring at her and couldn't say a word. He noticed that the room 'ad been altered, and that there was a big photygraph of her stuck up on the mantelpiece. He sat there fidgeting with 'is feet—until the 'ousekeeper looked at them—and then 'e got up and walked upstairs.

His uncle, wot was sitting on his bed when 'e went into the room and pretended that he 'adn't heard 'im come in, shook hands with 'im as though he'd never leave off.

"I've got something to tell you, Alf," he ses, arter they 'ad said "How d'ye do?" and he 'ad talked about the weather until Alf was fair tired of it.

"I've been and gone and done a foolish thing, and 'ow you'll take it I don't know."

"Been and asked the new 'ousekeeper to marry you, I s'pose?" ses Alf, looking at 'im very hard.

His uncle shook his 'ead. "I never asked 'er; I'd take my Davy I didn't," he ses.

"Well, you ain't going to marry her, then?" ses Alf, brightening up.

His uncle shook his 'ead agin. "She didn't want no asking," he ses, speaking very slow and mournful. "I just 'appened to put my arm round her waist by accident one day and the thing was done."

"Accident? How could you do it by accident?" ses Alf, firing up.

"How can I tell you that?" ses George Hatchard. "If I'd known 'ow, it wouldn't 'ave been an accident, would it?"

"Don't you want to marry her?" ses Alf, at last. "You needn't marry 'er if you don't want to."

George Hatchard looked at 'im and sniffed. "When you know her as well as I do you won't talk so foolish," he ses. "We'd better go down now, else she'll think we've been talking about 'er."

They went downstairs and 'ad tea together, and young Alf soon see the truth of his uncle's remarks. Mrs. Pearce—that was the 'ousekeeper's name—called his uncle "dear" every time she spoke to 'im, and arter tea she sat on the sofa side by side with 'im and held his 'and.

Alf lay awake arf that night thinking things over and 'ow to get Mrs.
Pearce out of the house, and he woke up next morning with it still on 'is mind. Every time he got 'is uncle alone he spoke to 'im about it, and told 'im to pack Mrs. Pearce off with a month's wages, but George Hatchard wouldn't listen to 'im.

"She'd 'ave me up for breach of promise and ruin me," he ses. "She reads the paper to me every Sunday arternoon, mostly breach of promise cases, and she'd 'ave me up for it as soon as look at me. She's got 'eaps and 'eaps of love-letters o' mine."

"Love-letters!" ses Alf, staring. "Love-letters when you live in the same house!"

"She started it," ses his uncle; "she pushed one under my door one morning, and I 'ad to answer it. She wouldn't come down and get my breakfast till I did. I have to send her one every morning."

"Do you sign 'em with your own name?" ses Alf, arter thinking a bit.

"No," ses 'is uncle, turning red.

"Wot do you sign 'em, then?" ses Alf.

"Never you mind," ses his uncle, turning redder. "It's my handwriting, and that's good enough for her. I did try writing backwards, but I only did it once. I wouldn't do it agin for fifty pounds. You ought to ha' heard 'er."

"If 'er fust husband was alive she couldn't marry you," ses Alf, very slow and thoughtful.

"No," ses his uncle, nasty-like; "and if I was an old woman she couldn't marry me. You know as well as I do that he went down with the Evening Star fifteen years ago."

"So far as she knows," ses Alf; "but there was four of them saved, so why not five? Mightn't 'e have floated away on a spar or something and been picked up? Can't you dream it three nights running, and tell 'er that you feel certain sure he's alive?"

"If I dreamt it fifty times it wouldn't make any difference," ses George Hatchard. "Here! wot are you up to? 'Ave you gone mad, or wot? You poke me in the ribs like that agin if you dare."

"Her fust 'usband's alive," ses Alf, smiling at 'im.

"Wot?" ses his uncle.

"He floated away on a bit o' wreckage," ses Alf, nodding at 'im, "just like they do in books, and was picked up more dead than alive and took to Melbourne. He's now living up-country working on a sheep station."

"Who's dreaming now?" ses his uncle.

"It's a fact," ses Alf. "I know a chap wot's met 'im and talked to 'im. She can't marry you while he's alive, can she?"

"Certainly not," ses George Hatchard, trembling all over; "but are you sure you 'aven't made a mistake?"

"Certain sure," ses Alf.

"It's too good to be true," ses George Hatchard.

"O' course it is," ses Alf, "but she won't know that. Look 'ere; you write down all the things that she 'as told you about herself and give it to me, and I'll soon find the chap I spoke of wot's met 'im. He'd meet a dozen men if it was made worth his while."

George Hatchard couldn't understand 'im at fust, and when he did he wouldn't 'ave a hand in it because it wasn't the right thing to do, and because he felt sure that Mrs. Pearce would find it out. But at last 'e wrote out all about her for Alf; her maiden name, and where she was born, and everything; and then he told Alf that, if 'e dared to play such a trick on an unsuspecting, loving woman, he'd never forgive 'im.

"I shall want a couple o' quid," ses Alf.

"Certainly not," ses his uncle. "I won't 'ave nothing to do with it, I tell you."

"Only to buy chocolates with," ses Alf.

"Oh, all right," ses George Hatchard; and he went upstairs to 'is bedroom and came down with three pounds and gave 'im. "If that ain't enough," he ses, "let me know, and you can 'ave more."

Alf winked at 'im, but the old man drew hisself up and stared at 'im, and then 'e turned and walked away with his 'ead in the air.

He 'ardly got a chance of speaking to Alf next day, Mrs. Pearce being 'ere, there, and everywhere, as the saying is, and finding so many little odd jobs for Alf to do that there was no time for talking. But the day arter he sidled up to 'im when the 'ouse-keeper was out of the room and asked 'im whether he 'ad bought the chocolates.

"Yes," ses Alfred, taking one out of 'is pocket and eating it, "some of 'em."

George Hatchard coughed and fidgeted about. "When are you going to buy the others?" he ses.

"As I want 'em," ses Alf. "They'd spoil if I got 'em all at once."

George Hatchard coughed agin. "I 'ope you haven't been going on with that wicked plan you spoke to me about the other night," he ses.

"Certainly not," ses Alf, winking to 'imself; "not arter wot you said. How could I?"

"That's right," ses the old man. "I'm sorry for this marriage for your sake, Alf. O' course, I was going to leave you my little bit of 'ouse property, but I suppose now it'll 'ave to be left to her. Well, well, I s'pose it's best for a young man to make his own way in the world."

"I s'pose so," ses Alf.

"Mrs. Pearce was asking only yesterday when you was going back to sea agin," ses his uncle, looking at 'im.

"Oh!" ses Alf.

"She's took a dislike to you, I think," ses the old man. "It's very 'ard, my fav'rite nephew, and the only one I've got. I forgot to tell you the other day that her fust 'usband, Charlie Pearce, 'ad a kind of a wart on 'is left ear. She's often spoke to me about it."

"In—deed!" ses Alf.

"Yes," ses his uncle, "left ear, and a scar on his forehead where a friend of his kicked 'im one day."

Alf nodded, and then he winked at 'im agin. George Hatchard didn't wink back, but he patted 'im on the shoulder and said 'ow well he was filling out, and 'ow he got more like 'is pore mother every day he lived.

"I 'ad a dream last night," ses Alf. "I dreamt that a man I know named Bill Flurry, but wot called 'imself another name in my dream, and didn't know me then, came 'ere one evening when we was all sitting down at supper, Joe Morgan and 'is missis being here, and said as 'ow Mrs. Pearce's fust husband was alive and well."

"That's a very odd dream," ses his uncle; "but wot was Joe Morgan and his missis in it for?"

"Witnesses," ses Alf.

George Hatchard fell over a footstool with surprise. "Go on," he ses, rubbing his leg. "It's a queer thing, but I was going to ask the Morgans 'ere to spend the evening next Wednesday."

"Or was it Tuesday?" ses Alf, considering.

"I said Tuesday," ses his uncle, looking over Alf's 'ead so that he needn't see 'im wink agin. "Wot was the end of your dream, Alf?"

"The end of it was," ses Alf, "that you and Mrs. Pearce was both very much upset, as o' course you couldn't marry while 'er fust was alive, and the last thing I see afore I woke up was her boxes standing at the front door waiting for a cab."

George Hatchard was going to ask 'im more about it, but just then Mrs. Pearce came in with a pair of Alf's socks that he 'ad been untidy enough to leave in the middle of the floor instead of chucking 'em under the bed. She was so unpleasant about it that, if it hadn't ha' been for the thought of wot was going to 'appen on Tuesday, Alf couldn't ha' stood it.

For the next day or two George Hatchard was in such a state of nervousness and excitement that Alf was afraid that the 'ousekeeper would notice it. On Tuesday morning he was trembling so much that she said he'd got a chill, and she told 'im to go to bed and she'd make 'im a nice hot mustard poultice. George was afraid to say "no," but while she was in the kitchen making the poultice he slipped out for a walk and cured 'is trembling with three whiskies. Alf nearly got the poultice instead, she was so angry.

She was unpleasant all dinner-time, but she got better in the arternoon, and when the Morgans came in the evening, and she found that Mrs. Morgan 'ad got a nasty sort o' red swelling on her nose, she got quite good-tempered. She talked about it nearly all supper-time, telling 'er what she ought to do to it, and about a friend of hers that 'ad one and 'ad to turn teetotaler on account of it.

"My nose is good enough for me," ses Mrs. Morgan, at last.

"It don't affect 'er appetite," ses George Hatchard, trying to make things pleasant, "and that's the main thing."

Mrs. Morgan got up to go, but arter George Hatchard 'ad explained wot he didn't mean she sat down agin and began to talk to Mrs. Pearce about 'er dress and 'ow beautifully it was made. And she asked Mrs. Pearce to give 'er the pattern of it, because she should 'ave one like it herself when she was old enough. "I do like to see people dressed suitable," she ses, with a smile.

"I think you ought to 'ave a much deeper color than this," ses Mrs. Pearce, considering.

"Not when I'm faded," ses Mrs. Morgan.

Mrs. Pearce, wot was filling 'er glass at the time, spilt a lot of beer all over the tablecloth, and she was so cross about it that she sat like a stone statue for pretty near ten minutes. By the time supper was finished people was passing things to each other in whispers, and when a bit o' cheese went the wrong way with Joe Morgan he nearly suffocated 'imself for fear of making a noise.

They 'ad a game o' cards arter supper, counting twenty nuts as a penny, and everybody got more cheerful. They was all laughing and talking, and Joe Morgan was pretending to steal Mrs. Pearce's nuts, when George Hatchard held up his 'and.

"Somebody at the street door, I think," he ses.

Young Alf got up to open it, and they 'eard a man's voice in the passage asking whether Mrs. Pearce lived there, and the next moment Alf came into the room, followed by Bill Flurry.

"Here's a gentleman o' the name o' Smith asking arter you," he ses, looking at Mrs. Pearce.

"Wot d'you want?" ses Mrs. Pearce rather sharp.

"It is 'er," ses Bill, stroking his long white beard and casting 'is eyes up at the ceiling. "You don't remember me, Mrs. Pearce, but I used to see you years ago, when you and poor Charlie Pearce was living down Poplar way."

"Well, wot about it?" ses Mrs. Pearce.

"I'm coming to it," ses Bill Flurry. "I've been two months trying to find you, so there's no need to be in a hurry for a minute or two. Besides, what I've got to say ought to be broke gently, in case you faint away with joy."

"Rubbish!" ses Mrs. Pearce. "I ain't the fainting sort."

"I 'ope it's nothing unpleasant," ses George Hatchard, pouring 'im out a glass of whisky.

"Quite the opposite," ses Bill. "It's the best news she's 'eard for fifteen years."

"Are you going to tell me wot you want, or ain't you?" ses Mrs. Pearce.

"I'm coming to it," ses Bill. "Six months ago I was in Melbourne, and one day I was strolling about looking in at the shop-winders, when all at once I thought I see a face I knew. It was a good bit older than when I see it last, and the whiskers was gray, but I says to myself—"

"I can see wot's coming," ses Mrs. Morgan, turning red with excitement and pinching Joe's arm.

"I ses to myself," ses Bill Flurry, "either that's a ghost, I ses or else it's Charlie—"

"Go on," ses George Hatchard, as was sitting with 'is fists clinched on the table and 'is eyes wide open, staring at 'im.

"Pearce," ses Bill Flurry.

You might 'ave heard a pin drop. They all sat staring at 'im, and then George Hatchard took out 'is handkerchief and 'eld it up to 'is face.

"But he was drownded in the Evening Star," ses Joe Morgan.

Bill Flurry didn't answer 'im. He poured out pretty near a tumbler of whisky and offered it to Mrs. Pearce, but she pushed it away, and, arter looking round in a 'elpless sort of way and shaking his 'ead once or twice, he finished it up 'imself.

"It couldn't 'ave been 'im," ses George Hatchard, speaking through 'is handkerchief. "I can't believe it. It's too cruel."

"I tell you it was 'im," ses Bill. "He floated off on a spar when the ship went down, and was picked up two days arterwards by a bark and taken to New Zealand. He told me all about it, and he told me if ever I saw 'is wife to give her 'is kind regards."

"Kind regards!" ses Joe Morgan, starting up. "Why didn't he let 'is wife know 'e was alive?"

"That's wot I said to 'im," ses Bill Flurry; "but he said he 'ad 'is reasons."

"Ah, to be sure," ses Mrs. Morgan, nodding. "Why, you and her can't be married now," she ses, turning to George Hatchard.

"Married?" ses Bill Flurry with a start, as George Hatchard gave a groan that surprised 'imself. "Good gracious! what a good job I found 'er!"

"I s'pose you don't know where he is to be found now?" ses Mrs. Pearce, in a low voice, turning to Bill.

"I do not, ma'am," ses Bill, "but I think you'd find 'im somewhere in Australia. He keeps changing 'is name and shifting about, but I dare say you'd 'ave as good a chance of finding 'im as anybody."

"It's a terrible blow to me," ses George Hatchard, dabbing his eyes.

"I know it is," ses Mrs. Pearce; "but there, you men are all alike. I dare say if this hadn't turned up you'd ha' found something else."

"Oh, 'ow can you talk like that?" ses George Hatchard, very reproachful. "It's the only thing in the world that could 'ave prevented our getting married. I'm surprised at you."

"Well, that's all right, then," ses Mrs. Pearce, "and we'll get married after all."

"But you can't," ses Alf.

"It's bigamy," ses Joe Morgan.

"You'd get six months," ses his wife.

"Don't you worry, dear," ses Mrs. Pearce, nodding at George Hatchard; "that man's made a mistake."

"Mistake!" ses Bill Flurry. "Why, I tell you I talked to 'im. It was Charlie Pearce right enough; scar on 'is forehead and a wart on 'is left ear and all."

"It's wonderful," ses Mrs. Pearce. "I can't think where you got it all from."

"Got it all from?" ses Bill, staring at her. "Why, from 'im."

"Oh, of course," ses Mrs. Pearce. "I didn't think of that; but that only makes it the more wonderful, doesn't it?—because, you see, he didn't go on the Evening Star."

"Wot?" ses George Hatchard. "Why you told me yourself—"

"I know I did," ses Mrs. Pearce, "but that was only just to spare your feelings. Charlie was going to sea in her, but he was prevented."

"Prevented?" ses two or three of 'em.

"Yes," ses Mrs. Pearce; "the night afore he was to 'ave sailed there was some silly mistake over a diamond ring, and he got five years. He gave a different name at the police-station, and naturally everybody thought 'e went down with the ship. And when he died in prison I didn't undeceive 'em."

She took out her 'andkerchief, and while she was busy with it Bill Flurry got up and went out on tiptoe. Young Alf got up a second or two arterwards to see where he'd gone; and the last Joe Morgan and his missis see of the happy couple they was sitting on one chair, and George Hatchard was making desprit and 'artrending attempts to smile.

AN ADULTERATION ACT

Dr. Frank Carson had been dreaming tantalizing dreams of cooling, effervescent beverages. Over and over again in his dreams he had risen from his bed, and tripping lightly down to the surgery in his pajamas, mixed himself something long and cool and fizzy, without being able to bring the dream to a satisfactory termination.

With a sudden start he awoke. The thirst was still upon him; the materials for quenching it, just down one flight of stairs. He would have smacked his lips at the prospect if they had been moist enough to smack; as it was, he pushed down the bedclothes, and throwing one leg out of bed- became firmly convinced that he was still dreaming.

For the atmosphere was stifling and odorous, and the ceiling descended in an odd bulging curve to within a couple of feet of his head. Still half asleep, he raised his fist and prodded at it in astonishment—a feeling which gave way to one of stupefaction as the ceiling took another shape and swore distinctly.

"I must be dreaming," mused the doctor; "even the ceiling seems alive."

He prodded it again-regarding it closely this time. The ceiling at once rose to greater altitudes, and at the same moment an old face with bushy whiskers crawled under the edge of it, and asked him profanely what he meant by it. It also asked him whether he wanted something for himself, because, if so, he was going the right way to work.

"Where am I?" demanded the bewildered doctor. "Mary! Mary!"

He started up in bed, and brought his head in sudden violent contact with the ceiling. Then, before the indignant ceiling could carry out its threat of a moment before, he slipped out of bed and stood on a floor which was in its place one moment and somewhere else the next.

In the smell of bilge-water, tar, and the foetid atmosphere generally his clouded brain awoke to the fact that he was on board ship, but resolutely declined to inform him how he got there. He looked down in disgust at the ragged clothes which he had on in lieu of the usual pajamas; and then, as events slowly pieced themselves together in his mind, remembered, as the last thing that he could remember, that he had warned his friend Harry Thomson, solicitor, that if he had any more to drink it would not be good for him.

He wondered dimly as he stood whether Thomson was there too, and walking unsteadily round the forecastle, roused the sleepers, one by one, and asked them whether they were Harry Thomson, all answering with much fluency in the negative, until he came to one man who for some time made no answer at all.

The doctor shook him first and then punched him. Then he shook him again and gave him little scientific slaps, until at length Harry Thomson, in a far-away voice, said that he was all right.

"Well, I'm glad I'm not alone," said the doctor, selfishly. "*Harry! Harry! Wake up!*"

"All ri'!" said the sleeper; "I'm all ri'!"

The doctor shook him again, and then rolled him backward and forward in his bunk. Under this gentle treatment the solicitor's faculties were somewhat brightened, and, half opening his eyes, he punched viciously at the disturber of his peace, until threatening voices from the gloom promised to murder both of them.

"Where are we?" demanded the doctor, of a deep voice from the other side of the forecastle which had been particularly threatening.

"Barque *Stella,* o' course," was the reply. "Where'd you think you was?"

The doctor gripped the edge of his friend's bunk and tried to think; then, a feeling of nausea overcoming all others, he clambered hurriedly up the forecastle ladder and lurched to the side of the vessel.

He leaned there for some time without moving, a light breeze cooling his fevered brow, and a small schooner some little distance from them playing seesaw, as he closed his eyes to the heaving blue sea. Land was conspicuous by its absence, and with a groan he turned and looked about him—at the white scrubbed deck, the snowy canvas towering aloft on lazily creaking spars, and the steersman leaning against the wheel regarding the officer who stood near by.

Dr. Carson, feeling a little better, walked sternly aft, the officer turning round and glancing in surprise at his rags as he approached.

"I beg your pardon," began the doctor, in superior tones.

"And what the devil do you want?" demanded the second officer; "who told you to come along here?"

"I want to know what this means," said the doctor, fiercely. "How dare you kidnap us on your beastly bilge-tank?"

"Man's mad," murmured the astonished second officer.

"Insufferable outrage!" continued the doctor. "Take us back to Melbourne at once."

"You get for'ard," said the other sharply; "get for'ard, and don't let me have any more of your lip."

"I want to see the captain of this ship," cried the doctor; "go and fetch him at once."

The second officer gazed at him, limp with astonishment, and then turned to the steersman, as though unable to believe his ears. The steersman pointed in front of him, and the other gave a cry of surprise and rage as he saw another tatterdemalion coming with uncertain steps toward him.

"Carson," said the new arrival, feebly; and coming closer to his friend, clung to him miserably.

"I'm just having it out with 'em, Thomson," said the doctor, energetically. "My friend here is a solicitor. Tell him what 'll happen if they don't take us back, Harry."

"You seem to be unaware, my good fellow," said the solicitor, covering a large hole in the leg of his trousers with his hand, "of the very dangerous situation in which you have placed yourselves. We have no desire to be harsh with you—"

"Not at all," acquiesced the doctor, nodding at the second officer.

"At the same time," continued Mr. Thomson—"at the—" He let go his friend's arm and staggered away; the doctor gazed after him sympathetically.

"His digestion is not all it should be," he said to the second officer, confidentially.

"If you don't get for'ard in two twos," said that gentleman, explosively, "I'll knock your heads off."

The doctor gazed at him in haughty disdain, and taking the limp Thomson by the arm, led him slowly away.

"How did we get here?" asked Mr. Harry Thomson, feebly.

The doctor shook his head.

"How did we get these disgusting clothes on?" continued his friend.

The doctor shook his head again. "The last thing I can remember, Harry," he said, slowly, "was imploring you not to drink any more."

"I didn't hear you," said the solicitor, crustily; "your speech was very indistinct last night."

"Seemed so to you, I dare say," said the other.

Mr. Thomson shook his arm off, and clinging to the mainmast, leaned his cheek against it and closed his eyes. He opened them again at the sound of voices, and drew himself up as he saw the second officer coming along with a stern-visaged man of about fifty.

"Are you the master of this vessel?" inquired the doctor, stepping to his friend's side.

"What the blazes has that got to do with you?" demanded the skipper. "Look here, my lads; don't you play any of your little games on me, because they won't do. You're both of you as drunk as owls."

"Defamation of character," said the solicitor, feebly, to his friend.

"Allow me," said the doctor, with his best manner, "to inquire what all this means. I am Dr. Frank Carson, of Melbourne; this gentleman is my friend Mr. Thomson, of the same place, solicitor."

"What?" roared the skipper, the veins in his forehead standing out. "Doctor! Solicitor! Why, you damned rascals, you shipped with me as cook and A. B."

"There's some mistake," said the doctor. "I'm afraid I shall have to ask you to take us back. I hope you haven't come far."

"Take those scarecrows away," cried the skipper, hoarsely; "take them away before I do them a mischief. I'll have the law of somebody for shipping two useless lubbers as seamen. Look to me like pickpockets."

"You shall answer for this," said Carson, foaming; "we're professional men, and we're not going to be abused by a bargee."

"Let him talk," said Mr. Thomson, hurriedly drawing his friend away from the irate skipper. "Let him talk."

"I'll put you both in quod when we get to Hong-kong," said the skipper. "Meantime, no work, no food; d'ye hear? Start and cook the breakfast, Mr. Doctor; and you. Mr. Lawyer, turn to and ask the boy to teach you an A. B's duties."

He walked back to the cabin; and the new cook was slowly pushed toward the galley by the second officer, the new A. B., under the same gentle guidance, being conducted back to the forecastle.

Fortunately for the new seamen the weather continued fine, but the heat of the galley was declared by the new cook to be insupportable. From the other hands they learned that they had been shipped with several others by a resourceful boarding-house master. The other hands, being men of plain speech, also said that they were brought aboard in a state of beastly and enviable intoxication, and chaffed crudely when the doctor attributed their apparent state of intoxication to drugs.

"You say you're a doctor?" said the oldest seaman.

"I am," said Carson, fiercely.

"Wot sort of a doctor are you, if you don't know when your licker's been played with, then?" asked the old man, as a grin passed slowly from mouth to mouth.

"I suppose it is because I drink so seldom," said the doctor, loftily. "I hardly know the taste of liquor myself, while as for my friend Mr. Thomson, you might almost call him a teetotaler."

"Next door to one," said the solicitor, who was sewing a patch on his trousers, as he looked up approvingly.

"You might call 'im a sailor, if you liked," said another seaman, "but that wouldn't make him one. All I can say is I never 'ad enough time or money to get in the state you was both in when you come aboard."

If the forecastle was incredulous, the cabin was worse. The officers at first took but little notice of them, but feeling their torn and tattered appearance was against them, they put on so many airs and graces to counteract this that flesh and blood could not endure it quietly. The cook would allude to his friend as Mr. Thomson, while the A. B. would persist in referring, with a most affected utterance, to Dr. Carson.

"Cook!" bawled the skipper one day when they were about a week out.

Dr. Carson, who was peeling potatoes, stepped slowly out of the galley and went toward him.

"You say 'Sir,' when you're spoken to," said the skipper, fiercely.

The doctor sneered.

"My — if you sneer at me, I'll knock your head off!" said the other, with a wicked look.

"When you get back to Melbourne," said the doctor, quietly, "you'll hear more of this."

"You're a couple of pickpockets aping the gentleman," said the skipper, and he turned to the mate. "Mr. Mackenzie, what do these two ragamuffins look like?"

"Pickpockets," said the mate, dutifully.

"It's a very handy thing," said the old man, jeeringly, "to have a doctor aboard. First time I've carried a surgeon."

Mr. Mackenzie guffawed loudly.

"And a solicitor," said the skipper, gazing darkly at the hapless Harry Thomson, who was cleaning brasswork. "Handy in case of disputes. He's a real sea lawyer. *Cook!*"

"Sir?" said the doctor, quietly.

"Go down and tidy my cabin, and see you do it well."

The doctor went below without a word, and worked like a housemaid. When he came on deck again, his face wore a smile almost of happiness, and his hand caressed one trousers pocket as though it concealed a hidden weapon.

For the following three or four days the two unfortunates were worked unceasingly. Mr. Thomson complained bitterly, but the cook wore a sphinx-like smile and tried to comfort him.

"It won't be for long, Harry," he said, consolingly.

The solicitor sniffed. "I could write tract after tract on temperance," he said, bitterly. "I wonder what our poor wives are thinking? I expect they have put us down as dead."

"Crying their eyes out," said the doctor, wistfully; "but they'll dry them precious quick when we get back, and ask all sorts of questions. What are you going to say, Harry?"

"The truth," said the solicitor, virtuously.

"So am I," said his friend; "but mind, we must both tell the same tale, whatever it is. Halloa! what's the matter?"

"It's the skipper," said the boy, who had just run up; "he wants to see you at once. He's dying."

He caught hold of the doctor by the sleeve; but Carson, in his most professional manner, declined to be hurried. He went leisurely down the companion-ladder, and met with a careless glance the concerned faces of the mate and second officer.

"Come to the skipper at once," said the mate.

"Does he want to see me?" said the doctor, languidly, as he entered the cabin.

The skipper was lying doubled up in his bunk, his face twisted with pain. "Doctor," he panted, "give me something quick. There's the medicine-chest."

"Do you want some food, sir?" inquired the other, respectfully.

"Food be damned!" said the sufferer. "I want physic. There's the medicine-chest." The doctor took it up and held it out to him. "I don't want the lot," moaned the skipper.

"I want you to give me something for red-hot corkscrews in the inside."

"I beg your pardon," said the doctor, humbly; "I'm only the cook."

"If you—don't—prescribe for me at once," said the skipper, "I'll put you in irons."

The doctor shook his head. "I shipped as cook," he said, slowly.

"Give me something, for Heaven's sake!" said the skipper, humbly. "I'm dying." The doctor pondered.

"If you dinna treat him at once, I'll break your skull," said the mate, persuasively.

The doctor regarded him scornfully, and turned to the writhing skipper.

"My fee is half a guinea a visit," he said, softly; "five shillings if you come to me."

"I'll have half a guinea's worth," said the agonized skipper.

The doctor took his wrist, and calmly drew the second officer's watch from its owner's pocket. Then he inspected the sick man's tongue, and shaking his head, selected a powder from the chest.

"You mustn't mind its being nasty," he said. "Where's a spoon?"

He looked round for one, but the skipper took the powder from his hand, and licked it from the paper as though it had been sherbet.

"For mercy's sake don't say it's cholera," he gasped.

"I won't say anything," said the doctor. "Where did you say the money was?"

The skipper pointed to his trousers, and Mr. Mackenzie, his national spirit rising in hot rage, took out the agreed amount and handed it to the physician.

"Am I in danger?" said the skipper.

"There's always danger," said the doctor, in his best bedside manner. "Have you made your will?"

The other, turning pale, shook his head. "Perhaps you'd like to see a solicitor?" said Carson, in winning tones.

"I'm not bad enough for that," said the skipper, stoutly.

"You must stay here and nurse the skipper, Mr. Mackenzie," said Carson, turning to the mate; "and be good enough not to make that snuffling noise; it's worrying to an invalid."

"Snuffling noise?" repeated the horror-struck mate.

"Yes; you've got an unpleasant habit of snuffling," said the doctor; "it sometimes. I worries me meant to speak to you about it before. You mustn't do it here. If you want to snuffle, go and snuffle on deck."

The frenzied outburst of the mate was interrupted by the skipper. "Don't make that noise in my cabin, Mr. Mackenzie," he said, severely.

Both mates withdrew in dudgeon, and Carson, after arranging the sufferer's bedclothes, quitted the cabin and sought his friend. Mr. Thomson was at first incredulous, but his eyes glistened brightly at the sight of the half-sovereign.

"Better hide it," he said, apprehensively; "the skipper 'll have it back when he gets well; it's the only coin we've got."

"He won't get well," said Dr. Carson, easily; "not till we get to Hong-kong, that is."

"What's the matter with him?" whispered the solicitor.

The doctor, evading his eye, pulled a long face and shook his head. "It may be the cooking," he said, slowly. "I'm not a good cook, I admit. It might be something got into the food from the medicine-chest. I shouldn't be at all surprised if the mates are taken bad too."

And indeed at that very moment the boy came rushing to the galley again, bawling out that Mr. Mackenzie was lying flat on his stomach in his bunk, punching the air with his fists and rending it with his language. The second officer appeared on deck as he finished his tale, and glancing forward, called out loudly for the cook.

"You're wanted, Frank," said the solicitor.

"When he calls me doctor, I'll go," said the other, stiffly.

"*Cook!*" bawled the second officer. "*Cook!* COOK!"

He came running forward, his face red and angry, and his fist doubled. "Didn't you hear me calling you?" he demanded, fiercely.

"I've been promoted," said Carson, sweetly. "I'm ship's surgeon now."

"Come down below at once, or I'll take you there by the scruff of your neck," vociferated the other.

"You're not big enough, little man," said the doctor, still smiling. "Well, well, lead the way, and we'll see what we can do."

He followed the speechless second officer below, and found the boy's description of the first officer's state as moonlight unto sunlight, as water unto wine. Even the second officer was appalled at the spectacle, and ventured a protest.

"Gie me something at once," yelled Mr. Mackenzie.

"Do you wish me to undertake your case?" inquired the doctor, suavely.

Mr. Mackenzie said that he did, in seven long, abusive, and wicked sentences.

"My fee is half a guinea," said the doctor, softly, poor people who cannot afford more, mates and the like, I sometimes treat for less."

"I'll die first," howled the mate; "you won't get any money out of me."

"Very good," said the doctor, and rose to depart.

"Bring him back, Rogers," yelled the mate; "don't let him go."

But the second officer, with a strange awesome look in his eyes, was leaning back in his seat, tightly gripping the edge of the table in both hands.

"Come, come," said the doctor, cheerily—"what's this? You mustn't be ill, Rogers. I want you to nurse these other two."

The other rose slowly to his feet and eyed him with lack-lustre eyes. "Tell the third officer to take charge," he said, slowly; "and if he's to he nurse as well, he's got his hands full."

The doctor sent the boy to apprise the third officer of his responsibilities, and then stood watching the extraordinary and snakelike convolutions of Mr. Mackenzie.

"How much—did—ye say?" hissed the latter.

"Poor people," repeated the doctor, with relish, "five shillings a visit; very poor people, half a crown."

"I'll have half a crown's worth," moaned the miserable mate.

"Mr. Mackenzie," said a faint voice from the skipper's cabin.

"Sir?" yelled the mate, who was in torment.

"Don't answer me like that, sir," said the skipper, sharply. "Will you please to remember that I'm ill, and can't bear that horrible noise you're making?"

"I'm—ill—too," gasped the mate.

"Ill? Nonsense!" said the skipper, severely. "We can't both be ill. How about the ship?"

There was no reply, but from another cabin the voice of Mr. Rogers was heard calling wildly for medical aid, and offering impossible sums in exchange for it. The doctor went from cabin to cabin, and, first collecting his fees, administered sundry potions to the sufferers; and then, in his capacity of cook, went forward and made an unsavory mess he called gruel, which he insisted upon their eating.

Thanks to his skill, the invalids were freed from the more violent of their pains, but this freedom was followed by a weakness so alarming that they could hardly raise their heads from their pillows—a state of things which excited the intense envy of the third officer, who, owing to his responsibilities, might just as well have been without one.

In this state of weakness, and with the fear of impending dissolution before his eyes, the skipper sent for Mr. Harry Thomson, and after some comparisons between lawyers and sharks, in which stress was laid upon certain redeeming features of the latter, paid a guinea and made his will. His example, save in the amount of the fee, was followed by the mate; but Mr. Rogers, being approached tentatively by the doctor in his friend's behalf, shook his head and thanked his stars he had nothing to leave. He had enjoyed his money, he said.

They mended slowly as they approached Hong-kong, though a fit of temper on Mr. Mackenzie's part, during which he threw out ominous hints about having his money back, led to a regrettable relapse in his case. He was still in bed when they came to anchor in the harbour; but the skipper and his second officer were able to go above and exchange congratulations from adjoining deck-chairs.

"You are sure it wasn't cholera?" asked the harbour-master's deputy, who had boarded them in his launch, after he had heard the story.

"Positive," said Carson.

"Very fortunate thing they had you on board," said the deputy—"very fortunate."

The doctor bowed.

"Seems so odd, the three of them being down with it," said the other; "looks as though it's infectious, doesn't it?"

"I don't think so," said the doctor, accepting with alacrity an offer to go ashore in the launch and change into some decent clothes. "I think I know what it was."

The captain of the *Stella* pricked up his ears, and the second officer leaned forward with parted lips. Carson, accompanied by the deputy and the solicitor, walked toward the launch.

"What was it?" cried the skipper, anxiously.

"I think that you ate something that disagreed with you," replied the doctor, grinning meaningly. "Good-by, captain."

The master of the *Stella* made no reply, but rising feebly, tottered to the side, and shook his fist at the launch as it headed for the shore. Doctor Carson, who had had a pious upbringing, kissed his hand in return.

AN ELABORATE ELOPEMENT

I have always had a slight suspicion that the following narrative is not quite true. It was related to me by an old seaman who, among other incidents of a somewhat adventurous career, claimed to have received Napoleon's sword at the battle of Trafalgar, and a wound in the back at Waterloo. I prefer to tell it in my own way, his being so garnished with nautical terms and expletives as to be half unintelligible and somewhat horrifying. Our talk had been of love and courtship, and after making me a present of several tips, invented by himself, and considered invaluable by his friends, he related this story of the courtship of a chum of his as illustrating the great lengths to which young bloods were prepared to go in his days to attain their ends.

It was a fine clear day in June when Hezekiah Lewis, captain and part owner of the schooner Thames, bound from London to Aberdeen, anchored off the little out-of-the-way town of Orford in Suffolk. Among other antiquities, the town possessed Hezekiah's widowed mother, and when there was no very great hurry—the world went slower in those days—the dutiful son used to go ashore in the ship's boat, and after a filial tap at his mother's window, which often startled the old woman considerably, pass on his way to see a young lady to whom he had already proposed five times without effect.

The mate and crew of the schooner, seven all told, drew up in a little knot as the skipper, in his shore-going clothes, appeared on deck, and regarded him with an air of grinning, mysterious interest.

"Now you all know what you have got to do?" queried the skipper.

"Ay, ay," replied the crew, grinning still more deeply.

Hezekiah regarded them closely, and then ordering the boat to be lowered, scrambled over the side, and was pulled swiftly towards the shore.

A sharp scream, and a breathless "Lawk-a-mussy me!" as he tapped at his mother's window, assured him that the old lady was alive and well, and he continued on his way until he brought up at a small but pretty house in the next road.

"Morning, Mr. Rumbolt," said he heartily to a stout, red-faced man, who sat smoking in the doorway.

"Morning, cap'n, morning," said the red-faced man.

"Is the rheumatism any better?" inquired Hezekiah anxiously, as he grasped the other's huge hand.

"So, so," said the other. "But it ain't the rheumatism so much what troubles me," he resumed, lowering his voice, and looking round cautiously. "It's Kate."

"What?" said the skipper.

"You've heard of a man being henpecked?" continued Mr. Rumbolt, in tones of husky confidence.

The captain nodded.

"I'm CHICK-PECKED" murmured the other.

"What?" inquired the astonished mariner again.

"Chick-pecked," repeated Mr. Rumbolt firmly. "CHIK-PEKED. D'ye understand me?"

The captain said that he did, and stood silent awhile, with the air of a man who wants to say something, but is half afraid to. At last, with a desperate appearance of resolution, he bent down to the old man's ear.

"That's the deaf 'un," said Mr. Rumbolt promptly.

Hezekiah changed ears, speaking at first slowly and awkwardly, but becoming more fluent as he warmed with his subject; while the expression of his listener's face gradually changed from incredulous bewilderment to one of uncontrollable mirth. He became so uproarious that he was fain to push the captain away from him, and lean back in his chair and choke and laugh until he nearly lost his breath, at which crisis a remarkably pretty girl appeared from the back of the house, and patted him with hearty good will.

"That'll do, my dear," said the choking Mr. Rumbolt. "Here's Captain Lewis."

"I can see him," said his daughter calmly. "What's he standing on one leg for?"

The skipper, who really was standing in a somewhat constrained attitude, coloured violently, and planted both feet firmly on the ground.

"Being as I was passing close in, Miss Rumbolt," said he, "and coming ashore to see mother"—

To the captain's discomfort, manifestations of a further attack on the part of Mr. Rumbolt appeared, but were promptly quelled by the daughter.

"Mother?" she repeated encouragingly,

"I thought I'd come on and ask you just to pay a sort o' flying visit to the Thames." "Thank you, I'm comfortable enough where I am," said the girl.

"I've got a couple of monkeys and a bear aboard, which I 'm taking to a menagerie in Aberdeen," continued the captain, "and the thought struck me you might possibly like to see 'em." "Well, I don't know," said the damsel in a flutter. "Is it a big bear?"

"Have you ever seen an elephant?" inquired Hezekiah cautiously.

"Only in pictures," replied the girl.

"Well, it's as big as that, nearly," said he.

The temptation was irresistible, and Miss Rumbolt, telling her father that she should not be long, disappeared into the house in search of her hat and jacket, and ten minutes later the brawny rowers were gazing their fill into her deep blue eyes as she sat in the stern of the boat, and told Lewis to behave himself.

It was but a short pull out to the schooner, and Miss Rumbolt was soon on the deck, lavishing endearments on the monkey, and energetically prodding the bear with a handspike to make him growl. The noise of the offended animal as he strove to get through the bars of his cage was terrific, and the girl was in the full enjoyment of it, when she became aware of a louder noise still, and, turning round, saw the seamen at the windlass.

"Why, what are they doing?" she demanded, "getting up anchor?"

"Ahoy, there!" shouted Hezekiah sternly. "What are you doing with that windlass?"

As he spoke, the anchor peeped over the edge of the bows, and one of the seamen running past them took the helm.

"Now then," shouted the fellow, "stand by. Look lively there with them sails."

Obeying a light touch of the helm, the schooner's bow-sprit slowly swung round from the land, and the crew, hauling lustily on the ropes, began to hoist the sails.

"What the devil are you up to?" thundered the skipper. "Have you all gone mad? What does it all mean?"

"It means," said one of the seamen, whose fat, amiable face was marred by a fearful scowl, "that we've got a new skipper."

"Good heavens, a mutiny!" exclaimed the skipper, starting melodramatically against the cage, and starting hastily away again. "Where's the mate?"

"He's with us," said another seaman, brandishing his sheath knife, and scowling fearfully. "He's our new captain."

In confirmation of this the mate now appeared from below with an axe in his hand, and, approaching his captain, roughly ordered him below.

"I'll defend this lady with my life," cried Hezekiah, taking the handspike from Kate, and raising it above his head.

"Nobody'll hurt a hair of her beautiful head," said the mate, with a tender smile.

"Then I yield," said the skipper, drawing himself up, and delivering the handspike with the air of a defeated admiral tendering his sword.

"Good," said the mate briefly, as one of the men took it.

"What!" demanded Miss Rumbolt excitedly, "aren't you going to fight them? Here, give me the handspike."

Before the mate could interfere, the sailor, with thoughtless obedience, handed it over, and Miss Rumbolt at once tried to knock him over the head. Being thwarted in this design by the man taking flight, she lost her temper entirely, and bore down like a hurricane on the remaining members of the crew who were just approaching.

They scattered at once, and ran up the rigging like cats, and for a few moments the girl held the deck; then the mate crept up behind her, and with the air of a man whose job exactly suited him, clasped her tightly round the waist, while one of the seamen disarmed her.

"You must both go below till we've settled what to do with you," said the mate, reluctantly releasing her.

With a wistful glance at the handspike, the girl walked to the cabin, followed slowly by the skipper.

"This is a bad business," said the latter, shaking his head solemnly, as the indignant Miss Rumbolt seated herself.

"Don't talk to me, you coward!" said the girl energetically.

The skipper started.

"I made three of 'em run," said Miss Rumbolt, "and you did nothing. You just stood still, and let them take the ship. I'm ashamed of you."

The skipper's defence was interrupted by a hoarse voice shouting to them to come on deck, where they found the mutinous crew gathered aft round the mate. The girl cast a look at the shore, which was now dim and indistinct, and turned somewhat pale as the serious nature of her position forced itself upon her.

"Lewis," said the mate.

"Well," growled the skipper.

"This ship's going in the lace and brandy trade, and if so be as you're sensible you can go with it as mate, d'ye hear?"

"An' s'pose I do; what about the lady?" inquired the captain.

"You and the lady'll have to get spliced," said the mate sternly. "Then there'll be no tales told. A Scotch marriage is as good as any, and we'll just lay off and put you ashore, and you can get tied up as right as ninepence."

"Marry a coward like that?" demanded Miss Rumbolt, with spirit; "not if I know it. Why, I'd sooner marry that old man at the helm."

"Old Bill's got three wives a'ready to my sartin knowledge," spoke up one of the sailors. "The lady's got to marry Cap'n Lewis, so don't let's have no fuss about it."

"I won't," said the lady, stamping violently.

The mutineers appeared to be in a dilemma, and, following the example of the mate, scratched their heads thoughtfully.

"We thought you liked him," said the mate, at last, feebly.

"You had no business to think," said Miss Rumbolt. "You are bad men, and you'll all be hung, every one of you; I shall come and see it." "The cap'n's welcome to her for me," murmured the helmsman in a husky whisper to the man next to him. "The vixen!"

"Very good," said the mate. "If you won't, you won't. This end of the ship'll belong to you after eight o'clock of a night. Lewis, you must go for'ard with the men."

"And what are you going to do with me after?" inquired the fair prisoner.

The seven men shrugged their shoulders helplessly, and Hezekiah, looking depressed, lit his pipe, and went and leaned over the side.

The day passed quietly. The orders were given by the mate, and Hezekiah lounged moodily about, a prisoner at large. At eight o'clock Miss Rumbolt was given the key of the state-room, and the men who were not in the watch went below.

The morning broke fine and clear with a light breeze, which, towards mid-day, dropped entirely, and the schooner lay rocking lazily on a sea of glassy smoothness. The sun beat fiercely down, bringing the fresh paint on the taffrail up in blisters, and sorely trying the tempers of the men who were doing odd jobs on deck.

The cabin, where the two victims of a mutinous crew had retired for coolness, got more and more stuffy, until at length even the scorching deck seemed preferable, and the girl, with a faint hope of finding a shady corner, went languidly up the companion-ladder.

For some time the skipper sat alone, pondering gloomily over the state of affairs as he smoked his short pipe. He was aroused at length from his apathy by the sound of the companion being noisily closed, while loud frightened cries and hurrying footsteps on deck announced that something extraordinary was happening. As he rose to his feet he was confronted by Kate Rumbolt, who, panting and excited, waved a big key before him.

"I've done it," she cried, her eyes sparkling.

"Done what?" shouted the mystified skipper.

"Let the bear loose," said the girl. "Ha, ha! you should have seen them run. You should have seen the fat sailor!"

"Let the—phew—let the—Good heavens! here's a pretty kettle of fish!" he choked.

"Listen to them shouting," cried the exultant Kate, clapping her hands. "Just listen."

"Those shouts are from aloft," said Hezekiah sternly, "where you and I ought to be."

"I've closed the companion," said the girl reassuringly.

"Closed the companion!" repeated Hezekiah, as he drew his knife. "He can smash it like cardboard, if the fit takes him. Go in here."

He opened the door of his state-room.

"Shan't!" said Miss Rumbolt politely.

"Go in at once!" cried the skipper. "Quick with you."

"Sha—" began Miss Rumbolt again. Then she caught his eye, and went in like a lamb. "You come too," she said prettily.

"I've got to look after my ship and my men," said the skipper. "I suppose you thought the ship would steer itself, didn't you?"

"Mutineers deserve to be eaten," whimpered Miss Rumbolt piously, somewhat taken aback by the skipper's demeanour.

Hezekiah looked at her.

"They're not mutineers, Kate," he said quietly. "It was just a piece of mad folly of mine. They're as honest a set of old sea dogs as ever breathed, and I only hope they are all safe up aloft. I'm going to lock you in; but don't be frightened, it shan't hurt you."

He slammed the door on her protests, and locked it, and, slipping the key of the cage in his pocket, took a firm grip of his knife, and, running up the steps, gained the deck. Then his breath came more freely, for the mate, who was standing a little way up the fore rigging, after tempting the bear with his foot, had succeeded in dropping a noose over its head. The brute made a furious attempt to extricate itself, but the men hurried down with other lines, and in a short space of time the bear presented much the same appearance as the lion in Aesop's Fables, and was dragged and pushed, a heated and indignant mass of fur, back to its cage.

Having locked up one prisoner the skipper went below and released the other, who passed quickly from a somewhat hysterical condition to one of such haughty disdain that the captain was thoroughly cowed, and stood humbly aside to let her pass.

The fat seaman was standing in front of the cage as she reached it, and regarding the bear with much satisfaction until Kate sidled up to him, and begged him, as a personal favour, to go in the cage and undo it.

"Undo it! Why he'd kill me!" gasped the fat seaman, aghast at such simplicity.

"I don't think he would," said his tormenter, with a bewitching smile; "and I'll wear a lock of your hair all my life if you do. But you'd better give it to me before you go in."

"I ain't going in," said the fat sailor shortly.

"Not for me?" queried Kate archly,

"Not for fifty like you," replied the old man firmly. "He nearly had me when he was loose. I can't think how he got out."

"Why, I let him out," said Miss Rumbolt airily. "Just for a little run. How would you like to be shut up all day?"

The sailor was just going to tell her with more fluency than politeness when he was interrupted. "That'll do," said the skipper, who had come behind them. "Go for'ard, you. There's been enough of this fooling; the lady thought you had taken the ship. Thompson, I'll take the helm; there's a little wind coming. Stand by there."

He walked aft and relieved the steersman, awkwardly conscious that the men were becoming more and more interested in the situation, and also that Kate could hear some of their remarks. As he pondered over the subject, and tried to think of a way out of it, the cause of all the trouble came and stood by him.

"Did my father know of this?" she inquired.

"I don't know that he did exactly," said the skipper uneasily. "I just told him not to expect you back that night."

"And what did he say?" said she.

"Said he wouldn't sit up," said the skipper, grinning, despite himself.

Kate drew a breath the length of which boded no good to her parent, and looked over the side.

"I was afraid of that traveller chap from Ipswich," said Hezekiah, after a pause. "Your father told me he was hanging round you again, so I thought I—well, I was a blamed fool anyway."

"See how ridiculous you have made me look before all these men," said the girl angrily.

"They've been with me for years," said Hezekiah apologetically, "and the mate said it was a magnificent idea. He quite raved about it, he did. I wouldn't have done it with some crews, but we've had some dirty times together, and they've stood by me well. But of course that's nothing to do with you. It's been an adventure I'm very sorry for, very."

"A pretty safe adventure for YOU," said the girl scornfully. "YOU didn't risk much. Look here, I like brave men. If you go in the cage and undo that bear, I'll marry you. That's what I call an adventure."

"Smith," called the skipper quietly, "come and take the helm a bit."

The seaman obeyed, and Lewis, accompanied by the girl, walked forward.

At the bear's cage he stopped, and, fumbling in his pocket for the key, steadily regarded the brute as it lay gnashing its teeth, and trying in vain to bite the ropes which bound it.

"You're afraid," said the girl tauntingly; "you're quite white."

The captain made no reply, but eyed her so steadily that her gaze fell. He drew the key from his pocket and inserted it in the huge lock, and was just turning it, when a soft arm was drawn through his, and a soft voice murmured sweetly in his ear, "Never mind about the old bear."

And he did not mind.

AN INTERVENTION

There was bad blood between the captain and mate who comprised the officers and crew of the sailing-barge "Swallow"; and the outset of their voyage from London to Littleport was conducted in glum silence. As far as the Nore they had scarcely spoken, and what little did pass was mainly in the shape of threats and abuse. Evening, chill and overcast, was drawing in; distant craft disappeared somewhere between the waste of waters and the sky, and the side-lights of neighbouring vessels were beginning to shine over the water. The wind, with a little rain in it, was unfavourable to much progress, and the trough of the sea got deeper as the waves ran higher and splashed by the barge's side.

"Get the side-lights out, and quick, you," growled the skipper, who was at the helm.

The mate, a black-haired, fierce-eyed fellow of about twenty-five, set about the task with much deliberation.

"And look lively, you lump," continued the skipper.

"I don't want none of your lip," said the mate furiously; "so don't you give me none."

The skipper yawned, and stretching his mighty frame laughed disagreeably. "You'll take what I give you, my lad," said he, "whether it's lip or fist."

"Lay a finger on me and I'll knife you," said the mate. "I ain't afraid of you, for all your size."

He put out the side-lights, casting occasional looks of violent hatred at the skipper, who, being a man of tremendous physique and rough tongue, had goaded his subordinate almost to madness.

"If you've done skulking," he cried, as he knocked the ashes out of his pipe, "come and take the helm."

The mate came aft and relieved him; and he stood for a few seconds taking a look round before going below. He dropped his pipe, and stooped to recover it; and in that moment the mate, with a sudden impulse, snatched up a handspike and dealt him a crashing blow on the head. Half-blinded and stunned by the blow, the man fell on his knees, and shielding his face with his hands, strove to rise. Before he could do so the mate struck wildly at him again, and with a great cry he fell backwards and rolled heavily overboard. The mate, with a sob in his breath, gazed wildly astern, and waited for him to rise. He waited: minutes seemed to pass, and still the body of the skipper did not emerge from the depths. He reeled back in a stupor; then he gave a faint cry as his eye fell on the boat, which was dragging a yard or two astern, and a figure which clung desperately to the side of it Before he had quite realised what had happened, he saw the skipper haul himself on to the stern of the boat and then roll heavily into it.

Panic-stricken at the sight, he drew his knife to cut the boat adrift, but paused as he reflected that she and her freight would probably be picked up by some passing vessel. As the thought struck him he saw the dim form of the skipper come towards the bow of the boat and, seizing the rope, begin to haul in towards the barge.

"Stop!" shouted the mate hoarsely; "stop! or I'll cut you loose."

The skipper let the rope go, and the boat pulled up with a jerk.

"I'm independent of you," the skipper shouted, picking up one of the loose boards from the bottom of the boat and brandishing it. "If there's any sea on I can keep her head to it with this. Cut away."

"If I let you come aboard," said the mate, "will you swear to let bygones be bygones?"

"No!" thundered the other. "Whether I come aboard or not don't make much difference. It'll be about twenty years for you, you murdering hound, when I get ashore."

The mate made no reply, but sat silently steering, keeping, however, a wary eye on the boat towing behind. He turned sick and faint as he thought of the consequences of his action, and vainly cast about in his mind for some means of escape.

"Are you going to let me come aboard?" presently demanded the skipper, who was shivering in his wet clothes.

"You can come aboard on my terms," repeated the mate doggedly.

"I'll make no terms with you," cried the other. "I hand you over to the police directly I get ashore, you mutinous dog. I've got a good witness in my head."

After this there was silence—silence unbroken through the long hours of the night as they slowly passed. Then the dawn came. The side-lights showed fainter and fainter in the water; the light on the mast shed no rays on the deck, but twinkled uselessly behind its glass. Then the mate turned his gaze from the wet, cheerless deck and heaving seas to the figure in the boat dragging behind. The skipper, who returned his gaze with a fierce scowl, was holding his wet handkerchief to his temple. He removed it as the mate looked, and showed a ghastly wound. Still, neither of them spoke. The mate averted his gaze, and sickened with fear as he thought of his position; and in that instant the skipper clutched the painter, and, with a mighty heave, sent the boat leaping towards the stern of the barge, and sprang on deck. The mate rose to his feet; but the other pushed him fiercely aside, and picking up the handspike, which lay on the raised top of the cabin, went below. Half an hour later he came on deck with a fresh suit of clothes on, and his head roughly bandaged, and standing in front of the mate, favoured him with a baleful stare.

"Gimme that helm," he cried.

The mate relinquished it.

"You dog!" snarled the other, "to try and kill a man when he wasn't looking, and then keep him in his wet clothes in the boat all night. Make the most o' your time. It'll be many a day before you see the sea again."

The mate groaned in spirit, but made no reply.

"I've wrote everything down with the time it happened," continued the other in a voice of savage satisfaction; "an' I've locked that handspike up in my locker. It's got blood on it."

"That's enough about it," said the mate, turning at last and speaking thickly. "What I've done I must put up with."

He walked forward to end the discussion; but the skipper shouted out choice bits from time to time as they occurred to him, and sat steering and gibing, a gruesome picture of vengeance.

Suddenly he sprang to his feet with a sharp cry. "There's somebody in the water," he roared; "stand by to pick him up."

As he spoke he pointed with his left hand, and with his right steered for something which rose and fell lazily on the water a short distance from them.

The mate, following his outstretched arm, saw it too, and picking up a boat-hook stood ready, until they were soon close enough to distinguish the body of a man supported by a life-belt.

"Don't miss him," shouted the skipper.

The mate grasped the rigging with one hand, and leaning forward as far as possible stood with the hook poised. At first it seemed as though the object would escape them, but a touch of the helm in the nick of time just enabled the mate to reach. The hook caught in the jacket, and with great care he gradually shortened it, and drew the body close to the side.

"He's dead," said the skipper, as he fastened the helm and stood looking down into the wet face of the man. Then he stooped, and taking him by the collar of his coat dragged the streaming figure on to the deck.

"Take the helm," he said.

"Ay, ay," said the other; and the skipper disappeared below with his burden.

A moment later he came on deck again. "We'll take in sail and anchor. Sharp there!" he cried.

The mate went to his assistance. There was but little wind, and the task was soon accomplished, and both men, after a hasty glance round, ran below. The wet body of the sailor lay on a locker, and a pool of water was on the cabin floor.

The mate hastily swabbed up the water, and then lit the fire and put on the kettle; while the skipper stripped the sailor of his clothes, and flinging some blankets in front of the fire placed him upon them.

For a long time they toiled in silence, in the faint hope that life still remained in the apparently dead body.

"Poor devil!" said the skipper at length, and fell to rubbing again.

"I don't believe he's gone," said the mate, panting with his exertions. "He don't feel like a dead man."

Ten minutes later the figure stirred slightly, and the men talked in excited whispers as they worked. A faint sigh came from the lips of the sailor, and his eyes partly opened.

"It's all right, matey," said the skipper; "you lie still; we'll do the rest. Jem, get some coffee ready."

By the time it was prepared the partly drowned man was conscious that he was alive, and stared in a dazed fashion at the man who was using him so roughly. Conscious that his patient was improving rapidly, the latter lifted him in his arms and placed him in his own bunk, and proffered him some steaming hot coffee. He sipped a little, then lapsed into unconsciousness again. The two men looked at each other blankly.

"Some of 'em goes like that." said the skipper. "I've seen it afore. Just as you think they're pulling round they slip their cable."

"We must keep him warm," said the mate. "I don't see as we can do any more."

"We'll get under way again," said the other; and pausing to heap some more clothes over the sailor he went on deck, followed by the mate; and in a short time the Swallow was once more moving through the water. Then the skipper, leaving the mate at the helm, went below.

Half an hour passed.

"Go and see what you can make of him," said the skipper as he re-appeared and took the helm. "He keeps coming round a bit, and then just drifts back. Seems like as if he can't hook on to life. Don't seem to take no interest in it."

The mate obeyed in silence; and for the remainder of the day the two men relieved each other at the bedside of the sailor. Towards evening, as they were entering the river which runs up to Littleport, he made decided progress under the skipper's ministrations; and the latter thrust his huge head up the hatchway and grinned in excusable triumph at the mate as he imparted the news. Then he suddenly remembered himself, and the smile faded. The light, too, faded from the mate's face.

"'Bout that mutiny and attempted murder," said the skipper, and paused as though waiting for the mate to contradict or qualify the terms; but he made no reply.

"I give you in charge as soon as we get to port," continued the other. "Soon as the ship's berthed, you go below."

"Ay, ay," said the mate, but without looking at him.

"Nice thing it'll be for your wife," said the skipper sternly. "You'll get no mercy from me."

"I don't expect none," said the mate huskily, "What I've done I'll stand to."

The reply on the skipper's lips merged into a grunt, and he went below. The sailor was asleep, and breathing gently and regularly; and after regarding him for some time the watcher returned to the deck and busied himself with certain small duties preparatory to landing.

Slowly the light faded out of the sky, and the banks of the river grew indistinct; and one by one the lights of Littleport came into view as they rounded the last bend of the river, and saw the little town lying behind its veil of masts and rigging. The skipper came aft and took the helm from the mate, and looked at him out of the corner of his eye, as he stood silently waiting with his hands by his side.

"Take in sail," said the skipper shortly; and leaving the helm a bit, ran to assist him. Five minutes later the Swallow was alongside of the wharf, and then, everything made fast and snug, the two men turned and faced each other.

"Go below," said the skipper sternly. The mate walked off. "And take care of that chap. I'm going ashore. If anybody asks you about these scratches, I got 'em in a row down Wapping—D'ye hear?"

The mate heard, but there was a thickness in his throat which prevented him from replying promptly. By the time he had recovered his voice the other had disappeared over the edge of the wharf, and the sound of his retreating footsteps rang over the cobblestone quay. The mate in a bewildered fashion stood for a short time motionless; then he turned, and drawing a deep breath, went below.

AN ODD FREAK

Speaking o' money," said the night-watchman thoughtfully, as he selected an empty soapbox on the wharf for a seat, "the whole world would be different if we all 'ad more of it. It would be a brighter and a 'appier place for everybody."

He broke off to open a small brass tobacco-box and place a little quid of tobacco tenderly into a pouch in his left cheek, critically observing at the same time the efforts of a somewhat large steamer to get alongside the next wharf without blocking up more than three parts of the river. He watched it as though the entire operation depended upon his attention, and, the steamer fast, he turned his eyes back again and resumed his theme.

"Of course it's the being short that sharpens people," he admitted thoughtfully; "the sharpest man I ever knew never 'ad a ha'penny in 'is pocket, and the ways 'e had o' getting other chaps to pay for 'is beer would ha' made 'is fortin at the law if 'e'd only 'ad the eddication. Playful little chap 'e was. I've seen men wot didn't know 'im stand 'im a pot o' beer and then foller 'im up the road to see 'im knock down a policeman as 'e'd promised. They'd foller 'im to the fust policeman 'e met, an' then 'e'd point them out and say they were goin' to half kill 'im, an' the policeman 'ud just stroll up an' ask 'em wot they were 'anging about for, but I never 'eard of a chap telling 'im. They used to go away struck all of a 'eap. He died in the accident ward of the London Horse-pittle, poor chap."

He shook his head thoughtfully, and ignoring the statement of a watchman at the next wharf that it was a fine evening, shifted his quid and laughed rumblingly.

"The funniest way o' raising the wind I ever 'eard of," he said in explanation, "was one that 'appened about fifteen years ago. I'd just taken my discharge as A.B. from the North Star, trading between here and the Australian ports, and the men wot the thing 'appened to was shipmates o' mine, although on'y firemen.

"I knows it's a true story, becos I was in it a little bit myself, and the other part I 'ad from all of 'em, and besides, they didn't see anything funny in it at all, or anything out of the way. It seemed to them quite a easy way o' making money, and I dessay if it 'ad come off all right I should have thought so too.

"In about a week arter we was paid off at the Albert Docks these chaps was all cleaned out, and they was all in despair, with a thirst wot wasn't half quenched and a spree wot was on'y in a manner o' speaking just begun, and at the end of that time they came round to a room wot I 'ad, to see wot could be done. There was four of 'em in all: old Sam Small, Ginger Dick, Peter Russet, and a orphan nevy of Sam's whose father and mother was dead. The mother 'ad been 'alf nigger an' 'alf Malay when she was living, and Sam was always pertickler careful to point out that his nevy took arter 'er. It was enough to make the pore woman turn in 'er grave to say so, but Sam used to say that 'e owed it to 'is brother to explain.

"'Wot's to be done?' ses Peter Russet, arter they'd all said wot miserable chaps they was, an' 'ow badly sailor-men was paid. 'We're all going to sign on in the Land's End, but she doesn't sail for a fortnight; wot's to be done in the meantime for to live?'

"'There's your watch, Peter,' ses old Sam, dreamy-like, 'and there's Ginger's ring. It's a good job you kep' that ring, Ginger. We're all in the same boat, mates, an' I on'y wish as I'd got something for the general good. It's 'aving an orphan nevy wot's kep' me pore.'

"'Stow it,' ses the nevy, short-like.

"'Everything's agin us,' ses old Sam. There's them four green parrots I brought from Brazil, all dead.'

"'So are my two monkeys,' ses Peter Russet, shaking 'is 'ead; 'they used to sleep with me, too.'

"They all shook their 'eads then, and Russet took Sam up very sharp for saying that p'r'aps if he 'adn't slep' with the monkeys they wouldn't ha' died. He said if Sam knew more about monkeys than wot 'e did, why didn't 'e put 'is money in them instead o' green parrots wot pulled their feathers out and died of cold.

"'Talking about monkeys,' ses Ginger Dick, interrupting old Sam suddenly, 'wot about young Beauty here?'

"'Well, wot about him?' ses the nevy, in a nasty sort o' way.

"'W'y, 'e's worth forty monkeys an' millions o' green parrots,' ses Ginger, starting up; 'an' here 'e is a-wasting of 'is opportunities, going about dressed like a Christian. Open your mouth, Beauty, and stick your tongue out and roll your eyes a bit.'

"'W'y not leave well alone, Ginger?' ses Russet; and I thought so too. Young Beauty was quite enough for me without that.

"'Ter 'blige me,' ses Ginger, anxiously, 'just make yourself as ugly as wot you can, Beauty.'

"'Leave 'im alone,' ses old Sam, as his nevy snarled at 'em. 'You ain't everybody's money yourself, Ginger.'

"'I tell you, mates,' ses Ginger, speaking very slow and solemn, 'there's a fortin in 'im. I was lookin' at 'im just now, trying to think who 'e reminded me of. At fust I thought it was that big stuffed monkey we saw at Melbourne, then I suddenly remembered it was a wild man of Borneo I see when I was a kid up in Sunderland. When I say 'e was a 'andsome, good-'arted looking gentleman alongside o' you, Beauty, do you begin to get my meaning?'

"'Wot's the idea, Ginger?' ses Sam, getting up to lend me and Russet a 'and with 'is nevy.

"'My idea is this,' ses Ginger; 'take 'is cloes off 'im and dress 'im up in that there winder-blind, or something o' the kind; tie 'im up with a bit o' line, and take 'im round to Ted Reddish in the 'Ighway and sell 'im for a 'undered quid as a wild man of Borneo.'

"'Wot?' screams Beauty, in an awful voice. 'Let go, Peter; let go, d'ye hear?'

"''Old your noise, Beauty, while your elders is speaking,' ses 'is uncle, and I could see 'e was struck with the idea.

"'You jest try dressing me up in a winder-blind,' ses his nevy, half-crying with rage.

"Listen to reason, Beauty,' ses Ginger; 'you'll 'ave your share of the tin; it'll only be for a day or two, and then when we've cleared out you can make your escape, and there'll be twenty-five pounds for each of us.'

"''Ow do you make that out, Ginger?' ses Sam, in a cold voice.

"'Fours into a 'undered,' ses Ginger.

"'Ho,' ses Sam. 'Ho, indeed. I wasn't aweer that 'e was your nevy, Ginger.'

"'Share and share alike.' ses Russet. 'It's a very good plan o' yours, Ginger.'

"Ginger holds 'is 'ead up and looks at 'im 'ard.

"'I thought o' the plan,' 'e ses, speaking very slow and deliberate. 'Sam's 'is uncle, and 'e's the wild man. Threes into a 'undered go—'

"'You needn't bother your fat 'ead adding up sums, Ginger,' ses Russet, very polite. 'I'm going to 'ave my share; else I'll split to Ted Reddish.'

"None of 'em said a word about me: two of 'em was sitting on my bed; Ginger was using a 'ankerchief o' mine wot 'e found in the fireplace, and Peter Russet 'ad 'ad a drink out o' the jug on my washstand, and yet they never even mentioned me. That's firemen all over, and that's 'ow it is they get themselves so disliked.

"It took 'em best part of an 'our to talk round young Beauty, an' the langwidge they see fit to use made me thankful to think that the parrots didn't live to larn it.

"You never saw anything like Beauty when they 'ad finished with 'im. If 'e was bad in 'is cloes, 'e was a perfeck horror without 'em. Ginger Dick faked 'im up beautiful, but there was no pleasing 'im. Fust he found fault with the winder-blind, which 'e said didn't fit; then 'e grumbled about going bare-foot, then 'e wanted somethink to 'ide 'is legs, which was natural considering the shape of 'em. Ginger Dick nearly lost 'is temper with 'im, and it was all old Sam could do to stop himself from casting 'im off forever. He was finished at last, and arter Peter Russet 'ad slipped downstairs and found a bit o' broken clothes-prop in the yard, and 'e'd been shown 'ow to lean on it and make a noise, Ginger said as 'ow if Ted Reddish got 'im for a 'undered pounds 'e'd get 'im a bargain.

"'We must 'ave a cab,' ses old Sam.

"'Cab?' ses Ginger. 'What for?'

"'We should 'ave half Wapping following us,' ses Sam. 'Go out and put your ring up, Ginger, and fetch a cab.'

"Ginger started grumbling, but he went, and presently came back with the cab and the money, and they all went downstairs leading the wild man by a bit o' line. They only met one party coming up, and 'e seemed to remember somethink 'e'd forgotten wot ought to be fetched at once.

"Ginger went out fust and opened the cab-door, and then stood there waiting becos at the last moment the wild man said the winder-blind was slipping down. They got 'im out at last, but before 'e could get in the cab was going up the road at ten miles an hour, with Ginger 'anging on to the door calling to it to stop.

"It came back at about a mile an' a 'alf an hour, an' the remarks of the cabman was eggstrordinary. Even when he got back 'e wouldn't start till 'e'd got double fare paid in advance; but they got in at last and drove off.

"There was a fine scene at Ted Reddish's door. Ginger said that if there was a bit of a struggle it would be a good advertisement for Ted Reddish, and they might p'r'aps get more than a 'undered, and all the three of 'em could do, they couldn't get the wild man out o' that cab, and the cabman was hopping about 'arf crazy. Every now and then they'd get the wild man 'arf out, and then he'd get in agin and snarl. 'E didn't seem to know when to leave off, and Ginger and the others got almost as sick of it as the cabman. It must ha' taken two years' wear out o' that cab, but they got 'im out at last, and Reddish's door being open to see what the row was about, they went straight in.

"'Wot's all this?' ses Reddish, who was a tall, thin man, with a dark moustache.

"It's a wild man o' Borneo,' ses Ginger, panting; 'we caught 'im in a forest in Brazil, an' we've come 'ere to give you the fust offer.'

"Ted Reddish was so surprised 'e couldn't speak at fust. The wild man seemed to take 'is breath away, and 'e looked in a 'elpless kind o' way at 'is wife, who'd just come down. She was a nice-lookin' woman, fat, with a lot o' yaller hair, and she smiled at 'em as though she'd known 'em all their lives.

"'Come into the parlour,' she ses, kindly, just as Ted was beginning to get 'is breath.

"They followed 'em in, and the wild man was just going to make hisself comfortable in a easy-chair, when Ginger give 'im a look, an' 'e curled up on the 'earthrug instead.

"''E ain't a very fine specimen,' ses Ted Reddish, at last.

"'It's the red side-whiskers I don't like,' ses his wife. 'Besides, who ever 'eard of a wild man in a collar an' necktie?'

"'You've got hold o' the wrong one,' ses Ted Reddish, afore Ginger Dick could speak up for hisself.

"'Oh, I beg your pardin,' ses Mrs. Reddish to Ginger, very polite. 'I thought it was funny a wild man should be wearing a collar. It's my mistake. That's the wild man, I s'pose, on the 'earthrug?'

"That's 'im, mum,' ses old Sam, very short.

"'He don't look wild enough,' ses Reddish.

"'No; 'e's much too tame,' ses 'is wife, shaking her yaller curls.

"The chaps all looked at each other then, and the wild man began to think it was time he did somethink; and the nearest thing 'andy being Ginger's leg, 'e put 'is teeth into it. Anybody might ha' thought Ginger was the wild man then, the way 'e went on, and Mrs. Reddish said that even if he so far forgot hisself as to use sich langwidge afore 'er, 'e oughtn't to before a poor 'eathen animal.

"'How much do you want for 'im?' ses Ted Reddish, arter Ginger 'ad got 'is leg away, and taken it to the winder to look at it.

"'One 'undered pounds,' ses old Sam.

"Ted Reddish looked at 'is wife, and they both larfed as though they'd never leave orf.

"'Why, the market price o' the best wild men is only thirty shillings,' ses Reddish, wiping 'is eyes. 'I'll give you a pound for 'im.'

"Old Sam looked at Russet, and Russet looked at Ginger, and then they all larfed.

"'Well, there's no getting over you, I can see that,' ses Reddish, at last. 'Is he strong?'

"'Strong? Strong ain't the word for it,' ses Sam.

"'Bring 'im to the back and let 'im 'ave a wrestle with one o' the brown bears, Ted,' ses 'is wife.

"''E'd kill it,' ses old Sam, hastily.

"'Never mind,' ses Reddish, getting up; 'brown bears is cheap enough.'

"They all got up then, none of 'em knowing wot to do, except the wild man, that is, and he got 'is arms tight round the leg o' the table.

"'Well,' ses Ginger, 'we'll be pleased for 'im to wrestle with the bear, but we must 'ave the 'un-dered quid fust, in case 'e injures 'isself a little.'

"Ted Reddish looked 'ard at 'im, and then he looked at 'is wife agin.

"'I'll just go outside and talk it over with the missus,' he ses, at last, and they both got up and went out.

"'It's all right,' ses old Sam, winking at Ginger.

"'Fair cop,' ses Ginger, who was still rubbing his leg. 'I told you it would be, but there's no need for Beauty to overdo it. He nearly 'ad a bit out o' my leg.'

"'A'right,' ses the wild man, shifting along the 'earthrug to where Peter was sitting; 'but it don't do for me to be too tame. You 'eard wot she said.'

"'How are you feeling, old man?' ses Peter, in a kind voice, as 'e tucked 'is legs away under 'is chair.

"'Gurr,' ses the wild man, going on all fours to the back of the chair, 'gur—wug—wug—'

"'Don't play the fool, Beauty,' ses Peter, with a uneasy smile, as he twisted 'is 'ead round. 'Call 'im off, Sam.'

"'Gurr,' ses the wild man, sniffing at 'is legs; 'gurr.'

"'Easy on, Beauty, it's no good biting 'im till they come back,' ses old Sam.

"'I won't be bit at all,' ses Russet, very sharp, 'mind that, Sam. It's my belief Beauty's gone mad.'

"'Hush,' ses Ginger, and they 'eard Ted Reddish and 'is wife coming back. They came in, sat down agin, and after Ted 'ad 'ad another good look at the wild man and prodded 'im all over an' looked at 'is teeth, he spoke up and said they'd decided to give a 'undered pun for 'im at the end o' three days if 'e suited.

"'I s'pose,' ses Sam, looking at the others, 'that we could 'ave a bit of it now to go on with?'

"'It's agin our way of doing business,' ses Ted Reddish. 'If it 'ud been a lion or a tiger we could, but wild men we never do.'

"'The thing is,' ses Mrs. Reddish, as the wild man started on Russet's leg and was pulled off by Sam and Ginger, 'where to put 'im.'

"'Why not put 'im in with the black leopard?' ses her 'usband.

"'There's plenty o' room in his cage,' says 'is wife thoughtfully, 'and it 'ud be company for 'im too.'

"'I don't think the wild man 'ud like that,' ses Ginger.

"'I'm sartain sure 'e wouldn't,' says old Sam, shaking 'is 'ead.

"'Well, we must put 'im in a cage by hisself, I s'pose,' ses Reddish, 'but we can't be put to much expense. I'm sure the money we spent in cat's meat for the last wild man we 'ad was awful.'

"'Don't you spend too much money on cat's meat for 'im,' ses Sam, "e'd very likely leave it. Bringing 'im 'ome, we used to give 'im the same as we 'ad ourselves, and he got on all right.'

"'It's a wonder you didn't kill 'im,' ses Reddish, severely. 'He'll be fed very different 'ere, I can tell you. You won't know 'im at the end o' three days.'

"'Don't change 'im too sudden,' ses Ginger, keeping 'is 'ead turned away from the wild man, wot wos trying to catch 'is eye. 'Cook 'is food at fust, 'cos 'e's been used to it.'

"'I know wot to give 'im,' ses Reddish, offhandedly. 'I ain't been in the line twenty-seven years for nothink. Bring 'im out to the back, an' I'll put 'im in 'is new 'ome.'

"They all got up and, taking no notice of the wild man's whispers, follered Ted Reddish and 'is wife out to the back, where all the wild beasts in the world seemed to 'ave collected to roar out to each other what a beastly place it was.

"'I'm going to put 'im in "'Appy Cottage" for a time,' says Reddish; 'lend a hand 'ere, William,' he says, beckoning to one of 'is men.

"'Is that "'Appy Cottage"?' ses old Sam, sniffing, as they got up to a nasty, empty cage with a chain and staple in the wall.

"Ted Reddish said it was.

"'Wot makes you call it that?' ses Sam.

"Reddish didn't seem to 'ear 'im, and it took all Ginger's coaxing to get Beauty to go in.

"'It's on'y for a day or two,' he whispers.

"'But 'ow am I to escape when you've got the brass?' ses the wild man.

"'We'll look arter that,' ses Ginger, who 'adn't got the least idea.

"The wild man 'ad a little show for the last time, jist to impress Ted Reddish, an' it was pretty to see the way William 'andled 'im. The look on the wild man's face showed as 'ow it was a revelashun to 'im. Then 'is three mates took a last look at 'im and went off.

"For the fust day Sam felt uneasy about 'im, and used to tell us tales about 'is dead brother which made us think Beauty was lucky to take arter 'is mother; but it wore off, and the next night, in the Admiral Cochrane, 'e put 'is 'ead on Ginger's shoulder, and wep' for 'appiness as 'e spoke of 'is nevy's home at "'Appy Cottage.'

"On the third day Sam was for going round in the morning for the money, but Ginger said it wasn't advisable to show any 'aste; so they left it to the evening, and Peter Russet wrote Sam a letter signed 'Barnum,' offering 'im two 'undered for the wild man, in case Ted Reddish should want to beat 'em down. They all 'ad a drink before they went in, and was smiling with good temper to sich an extent that they 'ad to wait a minute to get their faces straight afore going in.

"'Come in,' ses Reddish, and they follered 'im into the parler, where Mrs. Reddish was sitting in a armchair shaking 'er' ead and looking at the carpet very sorrowful.

"'I was afraid you'd come,' she ses, in a low voice.

"'So was I,' ses Reddish.

"'What for?' ses old Sam. It didn't look much like money, and 'e felt cross.

"'We've 'ad a loss,' ses Mrs. Reddish. She touched 'erself, and then they see she was all in black, and that Ted Reddish was wearing a black tie and a bit o' crape round 'is arm.

"'Sorry to 'ear it, mum,' ses old Sam.

"'It was very sudden, too,' ses Mrs. Reddish, wiping 'er eyes.

"'That's better than laying long,' ses Peter Russet, comforting like.

"Ginger Dick gives a cough. 'Twenty-five pounds was wot 'e'd come for; not to 'ear this sort o' talk.'

"'We've been in the wild-beast line seven-an'-twenty years,' ses Mrs. Reddish, 'and it's the fust time anythink of this sort 'as 'appened.'

"''Ealthy family, I s'pose,' ses Sam, staring.

"'Tell 'im, Ted,' ses Mrs. Reddish, in a 'usky whisper.

"'No, you,' ses Ted.

"'It's your place,' ses Mrs. Reddish.

"'A woman can break it better,' ses 'er 'usband.

"'Tell us wot?' ses Ginger, very snappish.

"Ted Reddish cleared 'is throat.

"'It wasn't our fault,' he ses, slowly, while Mrs. Reddish began to cry agin; 'gin'rally speak-in', animals is afraid o' wild men, and night before last, as the wild man wot you left on approval didn't seem to like "'Appy Cottage," we took 'im out an' put 'im in with the tiger.'

"'Put him in with the WOT?' ses the unfort'nit man's uncle, jumping off 'is chair.

"'The tiger,' ses Reddish. 'We 'eard something in the night, but we thought they was only 'aving a little bit of a tiff, like. In the morning I went down with a bit o' cold meat for the wild man, and I thought at first he'd escaped; but looking a little bit closer—'

"'Don't, Ted,' ses 'is wife. 'I can't bear it.'

"'Do you mean to tell me that the tiger 'as eat 'im?' screams old Sam.

"'Most of 'im,' ses Ted Reddish; 'but 'e couldn't ha' been much of a wild man to let a tiger get the better of 'im. I must say I was surprised.'

"'We both was,' ses Mrs. Reddish, wiping 'er eyes.

"You might ha' 'eard a pin drop; old Sam's eyes was large and staring, Peter Russet was sucking 'is teeth, an' Ginger was wondering wot the law would say to it—if it 'eard of it.

"'It's an unfortunit thing for all parties,' ses Ted Reddish at last, getting up and standing on the 'earthrug.

"''Orrible,' ses Sam, 'uskily. 'You ought to ha' known better than to put 'im in with a tiger. Wot could you expect? W'y, it was a mad thing to do.'

"'Crool thing,' ses Peter Russet.

"'You don't know the bisness properly,' ses Ginger, 'that's about wot it is. 'You should ha' known better than that.'

"'Well, it's no good making a fuss about it,' ses Reddish. It was only a wild man arter all, and he'd ha' died anyway, cos 'e wouldn't eat the raw meat we gave 'im, and 'is pan o' water was scarcely touched. He'd ha' starved himself anyhow. I'm sorry, as I said before, but I must be off; I've got an appointment down at the docks.'

"He moved towards the door; Ginger Dick gave Russet a nudge and whispered something and Russet passed it on to Sam.

"What about the 'undered quid?' ses pore Beauty's uncle, catching 'old o' Reddish as 'e passed 'im.

"'Eh?' ses Reddish, surprised—'Oh, that's off.'

"'Ho!' says Sam. 'Ho! is it? We want a 'undered quid off of you; an' wot's more, we mean to 'ave it.'

"'But the tiger's ate 'im,' says Mrs. Reddish, explaining.

"'I know that,' ses Sam, sharply. 'But 'e was our wild man, and we want to be paid for 'im. You should ha' been more careful. We'll give you five minutes; and if the money ain't paid by that time we'll go straight off to the police-station.'

"'Well, go,' ses Ted Reddish.

"Sam got up, very stern, and looked at Ginger.

"'You'll be ruined if we do,' ses Ginger.

"'All right,' ses Ted Reddish, comfortably.

"I'm not sure they can't 'ang you,' ses Russet.

"'I ain't sure either,' says Reddish; 'and I'd like to know 'ow the law stands, in case it 'appens agin.'

"'Come on, Sam,' ses Ginger; 'come straight to the police-station.'

"He got up, and moved towards the door. Ted Reddish didn't move a muscle, but Mrs. Reddish flopped on her knees and caught old Sam round the legs, and 'eld him so's 'e couldn't move.

"'Spare 'im,' she ses, crying.

"'Lea' go o' my legs, mum,' ses Sam.

"'Come on, Sam,' ses Ginger; 'come to the police.'

"Old Sam made a desperit effort, and Mrs. Reddish called 'im a crool monster, and let go and 'id 'er face on 'er husband's shoulder as they all moved out of the parlour, larfing like a mad thing with hysterics.

"They moved off slowly, not knowing wot to do, as, of course, they knew they daren't go to the police about it. Ginger Dick's temper was awful; but Peter Russet said they mustn't give up all 'ope— he'd write to Ted Reddish and tell 'im as a friend wot a danger 'e was in. Old Sam didn't say anything, the loss of his nevy and twenty-five pounds at the same time being almost more than 'is 'art could bear, and in a slow, melancholy fashion they walked back to old Sam's lodgings.

"'Well, what the blazes is up now?' ses Ginger Dick, as they turned the corner.

"There was three or four 'undered people standing in front of the 'ouse, and women's 'eads out of all the winders screaming their 'ardest for the police, and as they got closer they 'eard a incessant knocking. It took 'em nearly five minutes to force their way through the crowd, and then they nearly went crazy as they saw the wild man with 'alf the winder-blind missing, but otherwise well and 'arty, standing on the step and giving rat-a-tat-tats at the door for all 'e was worth.

"They never got to know the rights of it, Beauty getting so excited every time they asked 'im 'ow he got on that they 'ad to give it up. But they began to 'ave a sort of idea at last that Ted Reddish 'ad been 'aving a game with 'em, and that Mrs. Reddish was worse than wot 'e was."

ANGELS' VISITS

Mr. William Jobling leaned against his door-post, smoking. The evening air, pleasant in its coolness after the heat of the day, caressed his shirt-sleeved arms. Children played noisily in the long, dreary street, and an organ sounded faintly in the distance. To Mr. Jobling, who had just consumed three herrings and a pint and a half of strong tea, the scene was delightful. He blew a little cloud of smoke in the air, and with half-closed eyes corrected his first impression as to the tune being played round the corner.

"Bill!" cried the voice of Mrs. Jobling, who was washing-up in the tiny scullery.

"'Ullo!" responded Mr. Jobling, gruffly.

"You've been putting your wet teaspoon in the sugar-basin, and—well, I declare, if you haven't done it again."

"Done what?" inquired her husband, hunching his shoulders.

"Putting your herringy knife in the butter. Well, you can eat it now; I won't. A lot of good me slaving from morning to night and buying good food when you go and spoil it like that."

Mr. Jobling removed the pipe from his mouth. "Not so much of it," he commanded. "I like butter with a little flavor to it. As for your slaving all day, you ought to come to the works for a week; you'd know what slavery was then."

Mrs. Jobling permitted herself a thin, derisive cackle, drowned hurriedly in a clatter of tea-cups as her husband turned and looked angrily up the little passage.

"Nag! nag! nag!" said Mr. Jobling.

He paused expectantly.

"Nag! nag! nag! from morning till night," he resumed. "It begins in the morning and it goes on till bedtime."

"It's a pity—" began Mrs. Jobling.

"Hold your tongue," said her husband, sternly; "I don't want any of your back answers. It goes on all day long up to bedtime, and last night I laid awake for two hours listening to you nagging in your sleep."

He paused again.

"Nagging in your sleep," he repeated.

There was no reply.

"Two hours!" he said, invitingly; "two whole hours, without a stop."

"I 'ope it done you good," retorted his wife. "I noticed you did wipe one foot when you come in to-night."

Mr. Jobling denied the charge hotly, and, by way of emphasizing his denial, raised his foot and sent the mat flying along the passage. Honor satisfied, he returned to the door-post and, looking idly out on the street again, exchanged a few desultory remarks with Mr. Joe Brown, who, with his hands in his pockets, was balancing himself with great skill on the edge of the curb opposite.

His gaze wandered from Mr. Brown to a young and rather stylishly-dressed woman who was approaching—a tall, good-looking girl with a slight limp, whose hat encountered unspoken feminine criticism at every step. Their eyes met as she came up, and recognition flashed suddenly into both faces.

"Fancy seeing you here!" said the girl. "Well, this is a pleasant surprise."

She held out her hand, and Mr. Jobling, with a fierce glance at Mr. Brown, who was not behaving, shook it respectfully.

"I'm so glad to see you again," said the girl; "I know I didn't thank you half enough the other night, but I was too upset."

"Don't mention it," said Mr. Jobling, in a voice the humility of which was in strong contrast to the expression with which he was regarding the antics of Mr. Brown, as that gentleman wafted kisses to the four winds of heaven.

There was a pause, broken by a short, dry cough from the parlor window. The girl, who was almost touching the sill, started nervously.

"It's only my missis," said Mr. Jobling.

The girl turned and gazed in at the window. Mr. Jobling, with the stem of his pipe, performed a brief ceremony of introduction.

"Good-evening," said Mrs. Jobling, in a thin voice. "I don't know who you are, but I s'pose my 'usband does."

"I met him the other night," said the girl, with a bright smile; "I slipped on a piece of peel or something and fell, and he was passing and helped me up."

Mrs. Jobling coughed again. "First I've heard of it," she remarked.

"I forgot to tell you," said Mr. Jobling, carelessly. "I hope you wasn't hurt much, miss?"

"I twisted my ankle a bit, that's all," said the girl; "it's painful when I walk."

"Painful now?" inquired Mr. Jobling, in concern.

The girl nodded. "A little; not very."

Mr. Jobling hesitated; the contortions of Mr. Brown's face as he strove to make a wink carry across the road would have given pause to a bolder man; and twice his wife's husky little cough had sounded from the window.

"I s'pose you wouldn't like to step inside and rest for five minutes?" he said, slowly.

"Oh, thank you," said the girl, gratefully; "I should like to. It—it really is very painful. I ought not to have walked so far."

She limped in behind Mr. Jobling, and after bowing to Mrs. Jobling sank into the easy-chair with a sigh of relief and looked keenly round the room. Mr. Jobling disappeared, and his wife flushed darkly as he came back with his coat on and his hair wet from combing. An awkward silence ensued.

"How strong your husband is!" said the girl, clasping her hands impulsively.

"Is he?" said Mrs. Jobling.

"He lifted me up as though I had been a feather," responded the girl. "He just put his arm round my waist and had me on my feet before I knew where I was."

"Round your waist?" repeated Mrs. Jobling.

"Where else should I put it?" broke in her husband, with sudden violence.

His wife made no reply, but sat gazing in a hostile fashion at the bold, dark eyes and stylish hat of the visitor.

"I should like to be strong," said the latter, smiling agreeably over at Mr. Jobling.

"When I was younger," said that gratified man, "I can assure you I didn't know my own strength, as the saying is. I used to hurt people just in play like, without knowing it. I used to have a hug like a bear."

"Fancy being hugged like that!" said the girl. "How awful!" she added, hastily, as she caught the eye of the speechless Mrs. Jobling.

"Like a bear," repeated Mr. Jobling, highly pleased at the impression he had made. "I'm pretty strong now; there ain't many as I'm afraid of."

He bent his arm and thoughtfully felt his biceps, and Mrs. Jobling almost persuaded herself that she must be dreaming, as she saw the girl lean forward and pinch Mr. Jobling's arm. Mr. Jobling was surprised too, but he had the presence of mind to bend the other.

"Enormous!" said the girl, "and as hard as iron. What a prize-fighter you'd have made!"

"He don't want to do no prize-fighting," said Mrs. Jobling, recovering her speech; "he's a respectable married man."

Mr. Jobling shook his head over lost opportunities. "I'm too old," he remarked.

"He's forty-seven," said his wife.

"Best age for a man, in my opinion," said the girl; "just entering his prime. And a man is as old as he feels, you know."

Mr. Jobling nodded acquiescence and observed that he always felt about twenty-two; a state of affairs which he ascribed to regular habits, and a great partiality for the company of young people.

"I was just twenty-two when I married," he mused, "and my missis was just six months—"

"You leave my age alone," interrupted his wife, trembling with passion. "I'm not so fond of telling my age to strangers."

"You told mine," retorted Mr. Jobling, "and nobody asked you to do that. Very free you was in coming out with mine."

"I ain't the only one that's free," breathed the quivering Mrs. Jobling. "I 'ope your ankle is better?" she added, turning to the visitor.

"Much better, thank you," was the reply.

"Got far to go?" queried Mrs. Jobling.

The girl nodded. "But I shall take a tram at the end of the street," she said, rising.

Mr. Jobling rose too, and all that he had ever heard or read about etiquette came crowding into his mind. A weekly journal patronized by his wife had three columns regularly, but he taxed his memory in vain for any instructions concerning brown-eyed strangers with sprained ankles. He felt that the path of duty led to the tram-lines. In a somewhat blundering fashion he proffered his services; the girl accepted them as a matter of course.

Mrs. Jobling, with lips tightly compressed, watched them from the door. The girl, limping slightly, walked along with the utmost composure, but the bearing of her escort betokened a mind fully conscious of the scrutiny of the street.

He returned in about half an hour, and having this time to run the gauntlet of the street alone, entered with a mien which caused his wife's complaints to remain unspoken. The cough of Mr. Brown, a particularly contagious one, still rang in his ears, and he sat for some time in fierce silence.

"I see her on the tram," he said, at last "Her name's Robinson—Miss Robinson."

"In-deed!" said his wife.

"Seems a nice sort o' girl," said Mr. Jobling, carelessly. "She's took quite a fancy to you."

"I'm sure I'm much obliged to her," retorted his wife.

"So I—so I asked her to give you a look in now and then," continued Mr. Jobling, filling his pipe with great care, "and she said she would. It'll cheer you up a bit."

Mrs. Jobling bit her lip and, although she had never felt more fluent in her life, said nothing. Her husband lit his pipe, and after a rapid glance in her direction took up an old newspaper and began to read.

He astonished Mrs. Jobling next day by the gift of a geranium in full bloom. Surprise impeded her utterance, but she thanked him at last with some warmth, and after a little deliberation decided to put it in the bedroom.

Mr. Jobling looked like a man who has suddenly discovered a flaw in his calculations. "I was thinking of the front parlor winder," he said, at last.

"It'll get more sun upstairs," said his wife.

She took the pot in her arms, and disappeared. Her surprise when she came down again and found Mr. Jobling rearranging the furniture, and even adding a choice ornament or two from the kitchen, was too elaborate to escape his notice.

"Been going to do it for some time," he remarked.

Mrs. Jobling left the room and strove with herself in the scullery. She came back pale of face and with a gleam in her eye which her husband was too busy to notice.

"It'll never look much till we get a new hearthrug," she said, shaking her head. "They've got one at Jackson's that would be just the thing; and they've got a couple of tall pink vases that would brighten up the fireplace wonderful. They're going for next to nothing, too."

Mr. Jobling's reply took the form of uncouth and disagreeable growlings. After that phase had passed he sat for some time with his hand placed protectingly in his trouser-pocket. Finally, in a fierce voice, he inquired the cost.

Ten minutes later, in a state fairly evenly divided between pleasure and fury, Mrs. Jobling departed with the money. Wild yearnings for courage that would enable her to spend the money differently, and confront the dismayed Mr. Jobling in a new hat and jacket, possessed her on the way; but they were only yearnings, twenty-five years' experience of her husband's temper being a sufficient safeguard.

Miss Robinson came in the day after as they were sitting down to tea. Mr. Jobling, who was in his shirt-sleeves, just had time to disappear as the girl passed the window. His wife let her in, and after five remarks about the weather sat listening in grim pleasure to the efforts of Mr. Jobling to find his coat. He found it at last, under a chair cushion, and, somewhat red of face, entered the room and greeted the visitor.

Conversation was at first rather awkward. The girl's eyes wandered round the room and paused in astonishment on the pink vases; the beauty of the rug also called for notice.

"Yes, they're pretty good," said Mr. Jobling, much gratified by her approval.

"Beautiful," murmured the girl. "What a thing it is to have money!" she said, wistfully.

"I could do with some," said Mr. Jobling, with jocularity. He helped himself to bread and butter and began to discuss money and how to spend it. His ideas favored retirement and a nice little place in the country.

"I wonder you don't do it," said the girl, softly.

Mr. Jobling laughed. "Gingell and Watson don't pay on those lines," he said. "We do the work and they take the money."

"It's always the way," said the girl, indignantly; "they have all the luxuries, and the men who make the money for them all the hardships. I seem to know the name Gingell and Watson. I wonder where I've seen it?"

"In the paper, p'r'aps," said Mr. Jobling.

"Advertising?" asked the girl.

Mr. Jobling shook his head. "Robbery," he replied, seriously. "It was in last week's paper. Somebody got to the safe and got away with nine hundred pounds in gold and bank-notes."

"I remember now," said the girl, nodding. "Did they catch them?"

"No, and not likely to," was the reply.

Miss Robinson opened her big eyes and looked round with an air of pretty defiance. "I am glad of it," she said.

"Glad?" said Mrs. Jobling, involuntarily breaking a self-imposed vow of silence. "Glad?"

The girl nodded. "I like pluck," she said, with a glance in the direction of Mr. Jobling; "and, besides, whoever took it had as much right to it as Gingell and Watson; they didn't earn it."

Mrs. Jobling, appalled at such ideas, glanced at her husband to see how he received them. "The man's a thief," she said, with great energy, "and he won't enjoy his gains."

"I dare say—I dare say he'll enjoy it right enough," said Mr. Jobling, "if he ain't caught, that is."

"I believe he is the sort of man I should like," declared Miss Robinson, obstinately.

"I dare say," said Mrs. Jobling; "and I've no doubt he'd like you. Birds of a—"

"That'll do," said her husband, peremptorily; "that's enough about it. The guv'nors can afford to lose it; that's one comfort."

He leaned over as the girl asked for more sugar and dropped a spoonful in her cup, expressing surprise that she should like her tea so sweet. Miss Robinson, denying the sweetness, proffered her cup in proof, and Mrs. Jobling sat watching with blazing eyes the antics of her husband as he sipped at it.

"Sweets to the sweet," he said, gallantly, as he handed it back.

Miss Robinson pouted, and, raising the cup to her lips, gazed ardently at him over the rim. Mr. Jobling, who certainly felt not more than twenty-two that evening, stole her cake and received in return a rap from a teaspoon. Mr. Jobling retaliated, and Mrs. Jobling, unable to eat, sat looking on in helpless fury at little arts of fascination which she had discarded—at Mr. Jobling's earnest request—soon after their marriage.

By dint of considerable self-control, aided by an occasional glance from her husband, she managed to preserve her calm until he returned from seeing the visitor to her tram. Then her pent-up feelings found vent.

Quietly scornful at first, she soon waxed hysterical over his age and figure. Tears followed as she bade him remember what a good wife she had been to him, loudly claiming that any other woman would have poisoned him long ago. Speedily finding that tears were of no avail, and that Mr. Jobling seemed to regard them rather as a tribute to his worth than otherwise, she gave way to fury, and, in a fine, but unpunctuated passage, told him her exact opinion of Miss Robinson.

"It's no good carrying on like that," said Mr. Jobling, magisterially, "and, what's more, I won't have it."

"Walking into my house and making eyes at my 'usband," stormed his wife.

"So long as I don't make eyes at her there's no harm done," retorted Mr. Jobling. "I can't help her taking a fancy to me, poor thing."

"I'd poor thing her," said his wife.

"She's to be pitied," said Mr. Jobling, sternly. "I know how she feels. She can't help herself, but she'll get over it in time. I don't suppose she thinks for a moment we have noticed her—her—her liking for me, and I'm not going to have her feelings hurt."

"What about my feelings?" demanded his wife.

"You have got me," Mr. Jobling reminded her.

The nine points of the law was Mrs. Jobling's only consolation for the next few days. Neighboring matrons, exchanging sympathy for information, wished, strangely enough, that Mr. Jobling was their husband. Failing that they offered Mrs. Jobling her choice of at least a hundred plans for bringing him to his senses.

Mr. Jobling, who was a proud man, met their hostile glances as he passed to and from his work with scorn, until a day came when the hostility vanished and gave place to smiles. Never so many people in the street, he thought, as he returned from work; certainly never so many smiles.
 People came hurriedly from their back premises to smile at him, and, as he reached his door, Mr. Joe Brown opposite had all the appearance of a human sunbeam. Tired of smiling faces, he yearned for that of his wife. She came out of the kitchen and met him with a look of sly content. The perplexed Mr. Jobling eyed her morosely.

"What are you laughing at me for?" he demanded.

"I wasn't laughing at you," said his wife.

She went back into the kitchen and sang blithely as she bustled over the preparations for tea. Her voice was feeble, but there was a triumphant effectiveness about the high notes which perplexed the listener sorely. He seated himself in the new easy-chair—procured to satisfy the supposed aesthetic tastes of Miss Robinson—and stared at the window.

"You seem very happy all of a sudden," he growled, as his wife came in with the tray.

"Well, why shouldn't I be?" inquired Mrs. Jobling. "I've got everything to make me so."

Mr. Jobling looked at her in undisguised amazement.

"New easy-chair, new vases, and a new hearthrug," explained his wife, looking round the room. "Did you order that little table you said you would?"

"Yes," growled Mr. Jobling.

"Pay for it?" inquired his wife, with a trace of anxiety.

"Yes," said Mr. Jobling again.

Mrs. Jobling's face relaxed. "I shouldn't like to lose it at the last moment," she said. "You 'ave been good to me lately, Bill; buying all these nice things. There's not many women have got such a thoughtful husband as what I have."

"Have you gone dotty? or what?" inquired her bewildered husband.

"It's no wonder people like you," pursued Mrs. Jobling, ignoring the question, and smiling again as she placed three chairs at the table. "I'll wait a minute or two before I soak the tea; I expect Miss Robinson won't be long, and she likes it fresh."

Mr. Jobling, to conceal his amazement and to obtain a little fresh air walked out of the room and opened the front door.

"Cheer oh!" said the watchful Mr. Brown, with a benignant smile.

Mr. Jobling scowled at him.

"It's all right," said Mr. Brown. "You go in and set down; I'm watching for her."

He nodded reassuringly, and, not having curiosity enough to accept the other's offer and step across the road and see what he would get, shaded his eyes with his hand and looked with exaggerated anxiety up the road. Mr. Jobling, heavy of brow, returned to the parlor and looked hard at his wife.

"She's late," said Mrs. Jobling, glancing at the clock. "I do hope she's all right, but I should feel anxious about her if she was my gal. It's a dangerous life."

"Dangerous life!" said Mr. Jobling, roughly. "What's a dangerous life?"

"Why, hers," replied his wife, with a nervous smile. "Joe Brown told me. He followed her 'ome last night, and this morning he found out all about her."

The mention of Mr. Brown's name caused Mr. Jobling at first to assume an air of indifference; but curiosity overpowered him.

"What lies has he been telling?" he demanded.

"I don't think it's a lie, Bill," said his wife, mildly. "Putting two and two—"

"What did he say?" cried Mr. Jobling, raising his voice.

"He said, 'She—she's a lady detective,'" stammered Mrs. Jobling, putting her handkerchief to her unruly mouth.

"A tec!" repeated her husband. "A lady tec?"

Mrs. Jobling nodded. "Yes, Bill. She—she—she—"

"Well?" said Mr. Jobling, in exasperation.

"She's being employed by Gingell and Watson," said his wife.

Mr. Jobling sprang to his feet, and with scarlet face and clinched fists strove to assimilate the information and all its meaning.

"What—what did she come here for? Do you mean to tell me she thinks I took the money?" he said, huskily, after a long pause.

Mrs. Jobling bent before the storm. "I think she took a fancy to you, Bill," she said, timidly.

Mr. Jobling appeared to swallow something; then he took a step nearer to her. "You let me see you laugh again, that's all," he said, fiercely. "As for that Jezzybill—"

"There she is," said his wife, as a knock sounded at the door. "Don't say anything to hurt her feelings, Bill. You said she was to be pitied. And it must be a hard life to 'ave to go round and flatter old married men. I shouldn't like it."

Mr. Jobling, past speech, stood and glared at her. Then, with an inarticulate cry, he rushed to the front door and flung it open. Miss Robinson, fresh and bright, stood smiling outside. Within easy distance a little group of neighbors were making conversation, while opposite Mr. Brown awaited events.

"What d'you want?" demanded Mr. Jobling, harshly.

Miss Robinson, who had put out her hand, drew it back and gave him a swift glance. His red face and knitted brows told their own story.

"Oh!" she said, with a winning smile, "will you please tell Mrs. Jobling that I can't come to tea with her this evening?"

"Isn't there anything else you'd like to say?" inquired Mr. Jobling, disdainfully, as she turned away.

The girl paused and appeared to reflect. "You can say that I am sorry to miss an amusing evening," she said, regarding him steadily. "Good-by."

Mr. Jobling slammed the door.

BACK TO BACK

Mrs. Scutts, concealed behind the curtain, gazed at the cab in uneasy amazement. The cabman clambered down from the box and, opening the door, stood by with his hands extended ready for any help that might be needed. A stranger was the first to alight, and, with his back towards Mrs. Scutts, seemed to be struggling with something in the cab. He placed a dangling hand about his neck and, staggering under the weight, reeled backwards supporting Mr. Scutts, whose other arm was round the neck of a third man. In a flash Mrs. Scutts was at the door.

"Oh, Bill!" she gasped. "And by daylight, too!"

Mr. Scutts raised his head sharply and his lips parted; then his head sank again, and he became a dead weight in the grasp of his assistants.

"He's all right," said one of them, turning to Mrs. Scutts.

A deep groan from Mr. Scutts confirmed the statement.

"What is it?" inquired his wife, anxiously.

"Just a little bit of a railway accident," said one of the strangers. "Train ran into some empty trucks. Nobody hurt—seriously," he added, in response to a terrible and annoyed groan from Mr. Scutts.

With his feet dragging helplessly, Mr. Scutts was conveyed over his own doorstep and placed on the sofa.

"All the others went off home on their own legs," said one of the strangers, reproachfully. "He said he couldn't walk, and he wouldn't go to a hospital."

"Wanted to die at home," declared the sufferer. "I ain't going to be cut about at no 'ospitals."

The two strangers stood by watching him; then they looked at each other.

I don't want—no—'ospitals," gasped Mr. Scutts, "I'm going to have my own doctor."

"Of course the company will pay the doctor's bill," said one of the strangers to Mrs. Scutts or they'll send their own doctor. I expect he'll be all right to-morrow."

"I 'ope so," said Mr. Scutts, "but I don't think it. Thank you for bringing of me 'ome."

He closed his eyes languidly, and kept them closed until the men had departed.

"Can't you walk, Bill?" inquired the tearful Mrs. Scutts.

Her husband shook his head. "You go and fetch the doctor," he said, slowly. "That new one round the corner."

"He looks such a boy," objected Mrs. Scutts.

"You go and fetch 'im," said Mr. Scutts, raising his voice. "D'ye hear!"

"But—" began his wife.

"If I get up to you, my gal," said the forgetful Mr. Scutts, "you'll know it."

"Why, I thought—" said his wife, in surprise.

Mr. Scutts raised himself on the sofa and shook his fist at her. Then, as a tribute to appearances, he sank back and groaned again. Mrs. Scutts, looking somewhat relieved, took her bonnet from a nail and departed.

The examination was long and tedious, but Mr. Scutts, beyond remarking that he felt chilly, made no complaint. He endeavoured, but in vain, to perform the tests suggested, and even did his best to stand, supported by his medical attendant. Self-preservation is the law of Nature, and when Mr. Scutts's legs and back gave way he saw to it that the doctor was underneath.

"We'll have to get you up to bed," said the latter, rising slowly and dusting himself.

Mr. Scutts, who was lying full length on the floor, acquiesced, and sent his wife for some neighbours. One of them was a professional furniture-remover, and, half-way up the narrow stairs, the unfortunate had to remind him that he was dealing with a British working man, and not a piano. Four pairs of hands deposited Mr. Scutts with mathematical precision in the centre of the bed and then proceeded to tuck him in, while Mrs. Scutts drew the sheet in a straight line under his chin.

"Don't look much the matter with 'im," said one of the assistants.

"You can't tell with a face like that," said the furniture-remover. "It's wot you might call a 'appy face. Why, he was 'arf smiling as we, carried 'im up the stairs."

"You're a liar," said Mr. Scutts, opening his eyes.

"All right, mate," said the furniture-remover; "all right. There's no call to get annoyed about it. Good old English pluck, I call it. Where d'you feel the pain?"

"All over," said Mr. Scutts, briefly.

His neighbours regarded him with sympathetic eyes, and then, led by the furniture-remover, filed out of the room on tip-toe. The doctor, with a few parting instructions, also took his departure.

"If you're not better by the morning," he said, pausing at the door, "you must send for your club doctor."

Mr. Scutts, in a feeble voice, thanked him, and lay with a twisted smile on his face listening to his wife's vivid narrative to the little crowd which had collected at the front door. She came back, followed by the next-door neighbour, Mr. James Flynn, whose offers of assistance ranged from carrying Mr. Scutts out pick-a-back when he wanted to take the air, to filling his pipe for him and fetching his beer.

"But I dare say you'll be up and about in a couple o' days," he concluded. "You wouldn't look so well if you'd got anything serious the matter; rosy, fat cheeks and—"

"That'll do," said the indignant invalid. "It's my back that's hurt, not my face."

"I know," said Mr. Flynn, nodding sagely; "but if it was hurt bad your face would be as white as that sheet-whiter."

"The doctor said as he was to be kep' quiet," remarked Mrs. Scutts, sharply.

"Right-o," said Mr. Flynn. "Ta-ta, old pal. Keep your pecker up, and if you want your back rubbed with turps, or anything of that sort, just knock on the wall."

He went, before Mr. Scutts could think of a reply suitable for an invalid and, at the same time, bristling with virility. A sinful and foolish desire to leap out of bed and help Mr. Flynn downstairs made him more rubicund than ever.

He sent for the club doctor next morning, and, pending his arrival, partook of a basin of arrowroot and drank a little beef-tea. A bottle of castor-oil and an empty pill-box on the table by the bedside added a little local colour to the scene.

"Any pain?" inquired the doctor, after an examination in which bony and very cold fingers had played a prominent part.

"Not much pain," said Mr. Scutts. "Don't seem to have no strength in my back."

"Ah!" said the doctor.

"I tried to get up this morning to go to my work," said Mr. Scutts, "but I can't stand! couldn't get out of bed."

"Fearfully upset, he was, pore dear," testified Mrs. Scutts. "He can't bear losing a day. I s'pose—I s'pose the railway company will 'ave to do something if it's serious, won't they, sir?"

"Nothing to do with me," said the doctor. "I'll put him on the club for a few days; I expect he will be all right soon. He's got a healthy colour—a very healthy colour."

Mr. Scutts waited until he had left the house and then made a few remarks on the colour question that for impurity of English and strength of diction have probably never been surpassed.

A second visitor that day came after dinner—a tall man in a frock-coat, bearing in his hand a silk hat, which, after a careful survey of the room, he hung on a knob of the bedpost.

"Mr. Scutts?" he inquired, bowing.

"That's me," said Mr. Scutts, in a feeble voice.

"I've called from the railway company," said the stranger. "We have seen now all those who left their names and addresses on Monday afternoon, and I am glad to say that nobody was really hurt. Nobody."

Mr. Scutts, in a faint voice, said he was glad to hear it.

"Been a wonder if they had," said the other, cheerfully. "Why, even the paint wasn't knocked off the engine. The most serious damage appears to be two top-hats crushed and an umbrella broken."

He leaned over the bed-rail and laughed joyously. Mr. Scutts, through half-closed eyes, gazed at him in silent reproach.

"I don't say that one or two people didn't receive a little bit of a shock to their nerves," said the visitor, thoughtfully. "One lady even stayed in bed next day. However, I made it all right with them.

The company is very generous, and although of course there is no legal obligation, they made several of them a present of a few pounds, so that they could go away for a little change, or anything of that sort, to quiet their nerves."

Mr. Scutts, who had been listening with closed eyes, opened them languidly and said, "Oh."

"I gave one gentleman twen-ty pounds!" said the visitor, jingling some coins in his trouser-pocket. "I never saw a man so pleased and grateful in my life. When he signed the receipt for it—I always get them to sign a receipt, so that the company can see that I haven't kept the money for myself—he nearly wept with joy."

"I should think he would," said Mr. Scutts, slowly—"if he wasn't hurt."

"You're the last on my list," said the other, hastily. He produced a slip of paper from his pocket-book and placed it on the small table, with a fountain pen. Then, with a smile that was both tender and playful, he plunged his hand in his pocket and poured a stream of gold on the table.

"What do you say to thir-ty pounds?" he said, in a hushed voice. "Thirty golden goblins?"

"What for?" inquired Mr. Scutts, with a notable lack of interest.

"For—well, to go away for a day or two," said the visitor. "I find you in bed; it may be a cold or a bilious attack; or perhaps you had a little upset of the nerves when the trains kissed each other."

"I'm in bed—because—I can't walk-or stand," said Mr. Scutts, speaking very distinctly. "I'm on my club, and if as 'ow I get well in a day or two, there's no reason why the company should give me any money. I'm pore, but I'm honest."

"Take my advice as a friend," said the other; "take the money while you can get it."

He nodded significantly at Mr. Scutts and closed one eye. Mr. Scutts closed both of his.

"I 'ad my back hurt in the collision," he said, after a long pause. "I 'ad to be helped 'ome. So far it seems to get worse, but I 'ope for the best."

"Dear me," said the visitor; "how sad! I suppose it has been coming on for a long time. Most of these back cases do. At least all the doctors say so."

"It was done in the collision," said Mr. Scutts, mildly but firmly. "I was as right as rain before then."

The visitor shook his head and smiled. "Ah! you would have great difficulty in proving that," he said, softly; "in fact, speaking as man to man, I don't mind telling you it would be impossible. I'm afraid I'm exceeding my duty, but, as you're the last on my list, suppose—suppose we say forty pounds. Forty! A small fortune."

He added some more gold to the pile on the table, and gently tapped Mr. Scutts's arm with the end of the pen.

"Good afternoon," said the invalid.

The visitor, justly concerned at his lack of intelligence, took a seat on the edge of the bed and spoke to him as a friend and a brother, but in vain. Mr. Scutts reminded him at last that it was medicine-time, after which, pain and weakness permitting, he was going to try to get a little sleep.

"Forty pounds!" he said to his wife, after the official had departed. "Why didn't 'e offer me a bag o' sweets?"

"It's a lot o' money," said Mrs. Scutts, wistfully.

"So's a thousand," said her husband. "I ain't going to 'ave my back broke for nothing, I can tell you. Now, you keep that mouth o' yours shut, and if I get it, you shall 'ave a new pair o' boots."

"A thousand!" exclaimed the startled Mrs. Scutts. "Have you took leave of your senses, or what?"

"I read a case in the paper where a man got it," said Mr. Scutts. "He 'ad his back 'urt too, pore chap. How would you like to lay on your back all your life for a thousand pounds?"

"Will you 'ave to lay abed all your life?" inquired his wife, staring.

"Wait till I get the money," said Mr. Scutts; "then I might be able to tell you better."

He gazed wistfully at the window. It was late October, but the sun shone and the air was clear. The sound of traffic and cheerful voices ascended from the little street. To Mr. Scutts it all seemed to be a part of a distant past.

"If that chap comes round to-morrow and offers me five hundred," he said, slowly, "I don't know as I won't take it. I'm sick of this mouldy bed."

He waited expectantly next day, but nothing happened, and after a week of bed he began to realize that the job might be a long one. The monotony, to a man of his active habits, became almost intolerable, and the narrated adventures of Mr. James Flynn, his only caller, filled him with an uncontrollable longing to be up and doing.

The fine weather went, and Mr. Scutts, in his tumbled bed, lay watching the rain beating softly on the window-panes. Then one morning he awoke to the darkness of a London fog.

"It gets worse and worse," said Mrs. Scutts, as she returned home in the afternoon with a relish for his tea. "Can't see your 'and before your face."

Mr. Scutts looked thoughtful. He ate his tea in silence, and after he had finished lit his pipe and sat up in bed smoking.

"Penny for your thoughts," said his wife.

"I'm going out," said Mr. Scutts, in a voice that defied opposition. "I'm going to 'ave a walk, and when I'm far enough away I'm going to 'ave one or two drinks. I believe this fog is sent a-purpose to save my life."

Mrs. Scutts remonstrated, but in vain, and at half-past six the invalid, with his cap over his eyes and a large scarf tied round the lower part of his face, listened for a moment at his front door and then disappeared in the fog.

Left to herself, Mrs. Scutts returned to the bedroom and, poking the tiny fire into a blaze, sat and pondered over the willfulness of men.

She was awakened from a doze by a knocking at the street-door. It was just eight o'clock, and, inwardly congratulating her husband on his return to common sense and home, she went down and opened it. Two tall men in silk hats entered the room.

"Mrs. Scutts?" said one of them.

Mrs. Scutts, in a dazed fashion, nodded.

"We have come to see your husband," said the intruder. "I am a doctor."

The panic-stricken Mrs. Scutts tried in vain to think.

"He-he's asleep," she said, at last.

"Doesn't matter," said the doctor.

"Not a bit," said his companion.

"You—you can't see him," protested Mrs. Scutts. "He ain't to be seen."

"He'd be sorry to miss me," said the doctor, eyeing her keenly as she stood on guard by the inner door. "I suppose he's at home?"

"Of course," said Mrs. Scutts, stammering and flushing. "Why, the pore man can't stir from his bed."

"Well, I'll just peep in at the door, then," said the doctor. "I won't wake him. You can't object to that. If you do—"

Mrs. Scutts's head began to swim. "I'll go up and see whether he's awake," she said.

She closed the door on them and stood with her hand to her throat, thinking. Then, instead of going upstairs, she passed into the yard and, stepping over the fence, opened Mr. Flynn's back door.

"Halloa!" said that gentleman, who was standing in the scullery removing mud from his boots. "What's up?"

In a frenzied gabble Mrs. Scutts told him. "You must be 'im," she said, clutching him by the coat and dragging him towards the door. "They've never seen 'im, and they won't know the difference."

"But—" exclaimed the astonished James.

"Quick!" she said, sharply. "Go into the back room and undress, then nip into his room and get into bed. And mind, be fast asleep all the time."

Still holding the bewildered Mr. Flynn by the coat, she led him into the house and waved him upstairs, and stood below listening until a slight creaking of the bed announced that he had obeyed orders. Then she entered the parlour.

"He's fast asleep," she said, softly; "and mind, I won't 'ave him disturbed. It's the first real sleep he's 'ad for nearly a week. If you promise not to wake 'im you may just have a peep."

"We won't disturb him," said the doctor, and, followed by his companion, noiselessly ascended the stairs and peeped into the room. Mr. Flynn was fast asleep, and not a muscle moved as the two men approached the bed on tip-toe and stood looking at him. The doctor turned after a minute and led the way out of the room.

"We'll call again," he said, softly.

"Yes, sir," said Mrs. Scutts. "When?"

The doctor and his companion exchanged glances. "I'm very busy just at present," he said, slowly. "We'll look in some time and take our chance of catching him awake."

Mrs. Scutts bowed them out, and in some perplexity returned to Mr. Flynn. "I don't like the look of 'em," she said, shaking her head. "You'd better stay in bed till Bill comes 'ome in case they come back."

"Right-o," said the obliging Mr. Flynn. "Just step in and tell my landlady I'm 'aving a chat with Bill."

He lit his pipe and sat up in bed smoking until a knock at the front door at half-past eleven sent him off to sleep again. Mrs. Scutts, who was sitting downstairs, opened it and admitted her husband.

"All serene?" he inquired. "What are you looking like that for? What's up?"

He sat quivering with alarm and rage as she told him, and then, mounting the stairs with a heavy tread, stood gazing in helpless fury at the slumbering form of Mr. James Flynn.

"Get out o' my bed," he said at last, in a choking voice.

"What, Bill!" said Mr. Flynn, opening his eyes.

"Get out o' my bed," repeated the other. "You've made a nice mess of it between you. It's a fine thing if a man can't go out for 'arf a pint without coming home and finding all the riffraff of the neighbourhood in 'is bed."

"'Ow's the pore back, Bill?" inquired Mr. Flynn, with tenderness.

Mr. Scutts gurgled at him. "Outside!" he said as soon as he could get his breath.

"Bill," said the voice of Mrs. Scutts, outside the door.

"Halloa," growled her husband.

"He mustn't go," said Mrs. Scutts. "Those gentlemen are coming again, and they think he is you."

"WHAT!" roared the infuriated Mr. Scutts.

"Don't you see? It's me what's got the pore back now, Bill," said Mr. Flynn. "You can't pass yourself off as me, Bill; you ain't good-looking enough."

Mr. Scutts, past speech, raised his clenched fists to the ceiling.

"He'll 'ave to stay in your bed," continued the voice of Mrs. Scutts. "He's got a good 'art, and I know he'll do it; won't you, Jim?"

Mr. Flynn pondered. "Tell my landlady in the morning that I've took your back room," he said. "What a fortunit thing it is I'm out o' work. What are you walking up and down like that for, Bill? Back coming on agin?"

"Then o' course," pursued the voice of Mrs. Scutts, in meditative accents, "there's the club doctor and the other gentleman that knows Bill. They might come at any moment. There's got to be two Bills in bed, so that if one party comes one Bill can nip into the back room, and if the other Bill—party, I mean—comes, the other Bill—you know what I mean!"

Mr. Scutts swore himself faint.

"That's 'ow it is, mate," said Mr. Flynn. "It's no good standing there saying your little piece of poetry to yourself. Take off your clo'es and get to bed like a little man. Now! now! Naughty! Naughty!"

"P'r'aps I oughtn't to 'ave let 'em up, Bill," said his wife; "but I was afraid they'd smell a rat if I didn't. Besides, I was took by surprise."

"You get off to bed," said Mr. Scutts. "Get off to bed while you're safe."

"And get a good night's rest," added the thoughtful Mr. Flynn. "If Bill's back is took bad in the night I'll look after it."

Mr. Scutts turned a threatening face on him. "For two pins—" he began.

"For two pins I'll go back 'ome and stay there," said Mr. Flynn.

He put one muscular leg out of bed, and then, at the earnest request of Mr. Scutts, put it back again. In a few simple, manly words the latter apologized, by putting all the blame on Mrs. Scutts, and, removing his clothes, got into bed.

Wrapped in bedclothes, they passed the following day listening for knocks at the door and playing cards. By evening both men were weary, and Mr. Scutts made a few pointed remarks concerning dodging doctors and deceitful visitors to which Mr. Flynn listened in silent approval.

"They mightn't come for a week," he said, dismally. "It's all right for you, but where do I come in? Halves?"

Mr. Scutts had a rush of blood to the head.

"You leave it to me, mate," he said, controlling himself by an effort. "If I get ten quid, say, you shall have 'arf."

"And suppose you get more?" demanded the other.

"We'll see," said Mr. Scutts, vaguely.

Mr. Flynn returned to the charge next day, but got no satisfaction. Mr. Scutts preferred to talk instead of the free board and lodging his friend was getting. On the subject of such pay for such work he was almost eloquent.

"I'll bide my time," said Mr. Flynn, darkly. "Treat me fair and I'll treat you fair."

His imprisonment came to an end on the fourth day. There was a knock at the door, and the sound of men's voices, followed by the hurried appearance of Mrs. Scutts.

"It's *Jim's* lot," she said, in a hurried whisper. "I've just come up to get the room ready."

Mr. Scutts took his friend by the hand, and after warmly urging him not to forget the expert instructions he had received concerning his back, slipped into the back room, and, a prey to forebodings, awaited the result.

"Well, he looks better," said the doctor, regarding Mr. Flynn.

"Much better," said his companion.

Mrs. Scutts shook her head. "His pore back don't seem no better, sir," she said in a low voice. "Can't you do something for it?"

"Let me have a look at it," said the doctor. "Undo your shirt."

Mr. Flynn, with slow fingers, fumbled with the button at his neck and looked hard at Mrs. Scutts.

"She can't bear to see me suffer," he said, in a feeble voice, as she left the room.

He bore the examination with the fortitude of an early Christian martyr. In response to inquiries he said he felt as though the mainspring of his back had gone.

"How long since you walked?" inquired the doctor.

"Not since the accident," said Mr. Flynn, firmly.

"Try now," said the doctor.

Mr. Flynn smiled at him reproachfully.

"You can't walk because you think you can't," said the doctor; "that is all. You'll have to be encouraged the same way that a child is. I should like to cure you, and I think I can."

He took a small canvas bag from the other man and opened it. "Forty pounds," he said. "Would you like to count it?"

Mr. Flynn's eyes shone.

"It is all yours," said the doctor, "if you can walk across the room and take it from that gentleman's hand."

"Honour bright?" asked Mr. Flynn, in tremulous tones, as the other man held up the bag and gave him an encouraging smile.

"Honour bright," said the doctor.

With a spring that nearly broke the bed, Mr. Flynn quitted it and snatched the bag, and at the same moment Mrs. Scutts, impelled by a maddened arm, burst into the room.

"Your back!" she moaned. "It'll kill you Get back to bed."

"I'm cured, lovey," said Mr. Flynn, simply.

"His back is as strong as ever," said the doctor, giving it a thump.

Mr. Flynn, who had taken his clothes from a chair and was hastily dressing himself, assented.

"But if you'll wait 'arf a tick I'll walk as far as the corner with you," he said, quickly. "I'd like to make sure it's all right."

He paused at the foot of the stairs and, glancing up at the palid and murderous face of Mr. Scutts, which protruded from the back bedroom, smiled at him rapturously. Then, with a lordly air, he tossed him five pieces of gold.

W.W. Jacobs – A Short Biography

William Wymark Jacobs was born on September 8, 1863 in the Wapping district of London, England. An author, humorist and dramatist, Jacobs is best remembered for the enduring classic tale of horror - "The Monkey's Paw".

As a youth, Jacobs grew up near the Wapping docks in London, where his father was a wharf manager. The family's first home was home was a house on a River Thames wharf.

The docklands setting would show up frequently in his later literary output. Jacobs, the wharf rat, and his three siblings lost their mother when they were all still young children. Their father, William Gage Jacobs, remarried and fathered a further seven children with his erstwhile housekeeper Ellen Florey. Although he grew up surrounded by poverty, Jacobs himself received a formal education in London, first at a private prep school and later at the Birkbeck Literary and Scientific Institute (now part of the University of London and known as Birkbeck College).

Jacobs' adult working life began with a clerical position at the Post Office Savings Bank. The job was not a stimulating one but Jacobs put his imagination to good use and started to write short stories, sketches and articles, many of which appeared in the Post Office house publication "Blackfriars Magazine."

Although Jacobs did receive his fair share of rejection slips at the beginning of his career, many works written during this period of clerical employment appeared in the "Idler" and "Today" magazines, both of which were edited by noted humorist Jerome K. Jerome, who had taken a liking to Jacobs' stories.

From 1898, Jacobs also published stories in "The Strand", a popular, monthly fiction and general interest magazine. The arrangement stayed in place for most of his life and many of the works in Jacobs' subsequent collections – including the nautical serialization A Master of Craft (1899-1900) - appeared there first.

Jacobs' first volume of collected works was published in 1896. Many Cargoes, a selection of sea-faring yarns, established Jacobs as a popular writer and humorist with a penchant for authentic dialogue and trick endings (critics of the day referred to him as the "O. Henry of the Waterfront").

A year later he published a novelette, The Skipper's Wooing, and in 1898 and another collection of short stories titled Sea Urchins. These works painted vivid, if imaginatively stretched, pictures of dockland and seafaring London with colourful characters (such as "The Night Watchman", Ginger Dick) that now seem archetypal.

Many of Jacobs' periodical publications and first editions were illustrated with woodcuts and ink drawings, as was still the custom at the turn of the 20th century. The author worked regularly with artists such as E.W. Kemble, who had illustrated Mark Twain's Adventures of Huckleberry Finn and Harriet Beecher Stowe's Uncle Tom's Cabin, and his good friend Will Owen, who eventually became a household name on the strength of his iconic Bisto Kids, Bovril and Lux Soap advertising posters.

By 1899, Jacobs was able to quit the post office and finally begin a career making a living as a full-time writer.

He married the noted suffragist Agnes Eleanor Williams (who had been jailed for her protest activities) in 1900. They set up a household in Loughton, Essex as well as living part of the year in central London. The couple went on to have five children together though their marriage was considered an unhappy one.

The publication of two short novels: At Sunwich Port (a romantic tale of rival sea captains in the fictional seaside community of Sunwich standing in for the actual East England community of Sandwich, Kent) and Dialstone Lane (another small town romance involving intrigue and buried treasure), in 1902 and 1904 respectively, cemented Jacobs' reputation as one of the leading British authors of the new century.

On the foundations of a continuing ability to write for his audience he was readily published though he never strayed too far from what was becoming his familiar, dependable style. There followed a string of further successful publications, including Captain's All (1905), Night Watches (1914), The Castaways (1916), and Sea Whispers (1926). Jacobs published eighteen books in all during his lifetime; thirteen collections and five novels.

As a storyteller, Jacobs is perhaps better remembered for a handful of brief tales of the supernatural than for his popular nautical-themed works. The most famous of these, The Monkey's Paw, originally appeared as part of the 1902 short story collection The Lady of the Barge. It is an economically written story about a shriveled talisman, a monkey's paw that brings grief and horror in the wake of all too literal wish granting. The story has been adapted for other media repeatedly, starting with a one-act play performed at London's Haymarket Theatre in 1903. There have been multiple film adaptations of the story in the modern era; some of us are familiar with its appearance in an episode of the popular animated series, The Simpsons.

Another macabre gem, The Toll-House, was published as part of the collection Sailor's Knots in 1909. Jacob's once again employs a sparse style to tell the story of a group of men who spend the night in a famously haunted house on a dare (a noticeably similar narrative concept was put to use in the much earlier play The Ghost of Jerry Bundler, which had launched Jacobs' parallel career as a dramatist back in 1899 when it was produced at the St. James Theatre in London). Innovative at the time of writing, these sparingly written, atmospheric ghost stories are now familiar classics of the supernatural genre.

Though prolific in his younger years, Jacobs' productivity dropped dramatically after the start of World War I. Yet even in self-imposed semi-retirement Jacobs was still recognized as a leading humorist, ranked alongside such writers as P. G. Wodehouse and George Birmingham. He enjoyed continuing influence and elevated status among his fellow writers as evidenced by these comments attributed to his colleague Henry James:

"Mr. Jacobs, I envy you. You are popular! Your admirable work is appreciated by a wide circle of readers; it has achieved popularity. Mine never goes into a second edition."

James' literary fortunes would, of course, change, but his back-handedly complimentary admiration is compelling evidence of Jacobs' reputation as a writer and humourist both for his audience and his perhaps more admired literary colleagues.

Though Jacobs would create little in the way of new work after 1911, he was still writing. In these later years, seemingly burnt out creatively, Jacobs concentrated more on writing dramatizations and adaptations of his existing stories, including Beauty and the Barge (a film version starring Margaret Rutherford was also released in 1937) and In the Dark (a one act play that is often performed pr published with The Monkey's Paw adaptation).

Though admired by loyal readers throughout his lifetime, Jacobs has been almost completely forgotten since. Critics are at a loss to name a single reason why - Jacobs is universally considered to be a fine and imaginative literary craftsman. But, as critic John Wain suggested in a 1960 essay, perhaps Jacobs' humour may have been too gentle to persist into the cruel and sarcastic modern era, his dry pokes at proletariat hardship no longer suiting the times.

Nonetheless, Jacobs' legacy remains solid: he continued Dickens' (a writer with whom he is also often compared) tradition for sharing working class stories in authentic vernacular. And polished narratives such as The Monkey's Paw set a standard for the clever use of horror in fiction and popular culture that endures to this day. Indeed recently his works have begun to show an increased demand and appreciation in a world that is constantly looking over its shoulder.

William Wymark Jacobs died in a North London nursing home in Hornsey Lane, Islington on September 1st, 1943, just a week before his 80th birthday.

W.W. Jacobs – A Concise Bibliography

NOVELS AND SHORT STORY COLLECTIONS
MANY CARGOES (SHORT STORIES) (1896)
THE SKIPPER'S WOOING (1897)
SEA URCHINS (SHORT STORIES) (1898) aka MORE CARGOES

A MASTER OF CRAFT (1900)
LIGHT FREIGHTS (SHORT STORIES) (1901)
THE LADY OF THE BARGE (SHORT STORIES) (1902)
AT SUNWICH PORT (1902)
DIALSTONE LANE (1902)
SALTHAVEN (1908)
CAPTAINS ALL (SHORT STORIES) (1911)
NIGHT WATCHERS (SHORT STORIES) (1914)
DEEP WATERS (SHORT STORIES) (1919)

SHORT STORIES (INCLUDING THOSE USED IN THE COLLECTIONS ABOVE)
A BENEFIT PERFORMANCE
A BLACK AFFAIR
A CASE OF DESERTION
A CHANGE OF TREATMENT
A CIRCULAR TOUR
A DISCIPLINARIAN
A DISTANT RELATIVE
A GARDEN PLOT
A GOLDEN VENTURE
A HARBOUR OF REFUGE
A LOVE KNOT
A LOVE PASSAGE
A MARKED MAN
A MIXED PROPOSAL
A RASH EXPERIMENT
A SAFETY MATCH
A SPIRIT OF AVARICE
A TIGER'S SKIN
ADMIRAL PETERS
AFTER THE INQUEST
ALF'S DREAM
AN ADULTERATION ACT
AN ELABORATE ELOPEMENT
AN INTERVENTION
AN ODD FREAK
ANGELS' VISITS
BACK TO BACK
BEDRIDDEN
THE WINTER OFFENSIVE
THE BEQUEST
BILL'S LAPSE
BILL'S PAPER CHASE
BLUNDELL'S IMPROVEMENT
THE BOATSWAIN'S WATCH
THE BOATSWAIN'S MATE
BOB'S REDEMPTION
BREAKING A SPELL
BREVET RANK
BROTHER HUTCHINS

THE MADNESS OF MR. LISTER
"MANNERS MAKYTH MAN"
MATED
"MATRIMONIAL OPENINGS"
MIXED RELATIONS
MONEY CHANGERS
THE MONEY-BOX
THE MONKEY'S PAW
MRS. BUNKER'S CHAPERON
THE NEST EGG
ODD MAN OUT
THE OLD MAN OF THE SEA
OUTSAILED
OVER THE SIDE
PAYING OFF
THE PERSECUTION OF BOB PRETTY
PETER'S PENCE
PICKLED HERRING
PRIVATE CLOTHES
PRIZE MONEY
THE RESURRECTION OF MR. WIGGETT
THE RIVAL BEAUTIES
RULE OF THREE
SAM'S BOY
SAM'S GHOST
SELF-HELP
SENTENCE DEFERRED
SHAREHOLDERS
SKILLED ASSISTANCE
THE SKIPPER OF THE "OSPREY"
SMOKED SKIPPER
STEPPING BACKWARDS
STRIKING HARD
THE SUBSTITUTE
THE TEMPTATION OF SAMUEL BURGE
THE TEST
THE THREE SISTERS
TO HAVE AND TO HOLD
"THE TOLL-HOUSE"
TWIN SPIRITS
TWO OF A TRADE
THE UNDERSTUDY
THE UNKNOWN
THE VIGIL
WATCH-DOGS
THE WEAKER VESSEL
THE WELL
THE WHITE CAT

STAGE

THE GHOST OF JERRY BUNDLER (1899) (In London)